# Murder All Sewn Up

(A Spicetown Spin-Off)

A Carom Seed Cozy

Sheri Richey

Sheri Richey



For further information, contact the publisher: Cagelink



ISBN: 9781648715020

Front Cover art by Mariah Sinclair

# Spicetown Mysteries

Welcome to Spicetown

A Bell in the Garden

Spilling the Spice

Blue Collar Bluff

A Tough Nut to Crack

Chicory is Trickery

The No Dill Zone

Cons & Quinces

Silent Night Dynamite

# Keslar Mansion Mysteries

(A Spicetown Spin-off)

Cat In Cahoots

Cat Incognito

Cat In Control

Sheri Richey

Romance by Sheri Richey:

The Eden Hall Series:
Finding Eden
Saving Eden
Healing Eden
Protecting Eden
Completing Eden
∞
Willow Wood
Knight Events

Sheri Richey

# Chapter 1

Arlene Emery skittered across Fennel Street in the misting rain, seeking coverage under the awning of the Carom Seed Craft Corner and rummaged in her handbag for the door key. It was after nine o'clock and the closed sign was still in the window. Hoping she had not forgotten that she was opening today, she unlocked the door to the darkened store.

"Peggy?" Shouting toward the back room where she saw a light on, Arlene draped her coat over the back of the chair behind the counter and flipped the store front lights on before turning the closed sign to open. "Are you back there?"

"Yeah, I'm here."

Arlene heard the rustle of packing paper

being pulled from boxes and peered around the corner of the storage room. Peggy was hunched over a large supply box, pulling out bags of ribbon and thread that needed to be put out for display.

"I'm just checking over the packing list on the shipments we got yesterday. They didn't send the glue sticks again. They're on back order. I've got to find a different vendor."

Arlene reached for the brown crumpled paper strewn across the room. Running her hand over it to smooth out the wrinkles, she folded it into a neat square. "I'll go finish unpacking the pattern boxes up front. Do you want me to pull the winter fabric so we can put out the new spring stuff?"

Peggy stood up and wrinkled her nose. Although it was spring by the calendar, the weatherman had missed the memo. "Let's wait a week for that."

Arlene nodded and cocked her head. "Did you hear something?"

Peggy looked around the storage room. The

overhead rolling door used for large deliveries was up and the light patter of rain could be heard falling on the graveled alley behind the store. "I don't hear anything except rain."

Arlene looked at the floor and saw a mountain of packing paper move an inch to the left. Shrieking, she stepped back and pointed. "Did you see that? That paper is moving!"

Peggy glanced at the mound of brown paper. "I don't see anything." Reaching around the box she grabbed the top piece and waded it into a ball.

"There! Did you hear that? It's a squeak!" Arlene stepped back slowly. "Oh no, is there a mouse in here?"

"If there is, I'll run it outside. Don't worry. Let me clean this up and get the box into the dumpster." Peggy grabbed the packing paper and shoved it into the empty box as Arlene eyed the room with suspicion.

Arlene flattened her hand over her chest. "That's a whimper! That's not a mouse." Tossing paper in the air left and right to clear the debris from the floor, the whining increased as Arlene uncovered the source of the sound. “Look!”

Peggy scowled down at the tiny wet puppy shivering from cold or fear. “Where did that come from?”

“Ah, baby,” Arlene cooed and scooped the little wobbly pup into her arms. “Do we have a towel?”

Peggy looked around the room. “No.”

Arlene huffed and carried him into the restroom to grab some paper towels. “He’s so cold, bless his heart. He must have been dumped in the alley.”

“He can’t stay here.” Peggy shook her head vigorously. “We can’t have a dog in here.”

“He won’t hurt anything. We’ll find him a home.” Arlene kissed his head and wrapped both arms around him for warmth.

“You need to take him to the shelter.” Peggy grabbed the paper from the floor and smashed it down into the empty boxes. “Shelby will find it a home.”

“They don’t open until ten,” Arlene smirked.

Shelby Worth ran the Spicetown Animal Shelter and Arlene had adopted her dog and cat from there. "And he needs to see a veterinarian first. He's very small and scared. How could anyone abandon a little baby like this? We need to look around the alley and make sure there aren't more puppies or a mother dog out there. Did you see anything when you drove up this morning?"

"No, but I wasn't looking. What are you going to do with it? It can't stay here." Peggy dragged the boxes out into the alley and flung them into the dumpster, hopping over puddles as she hurried back through the delivery door.

"I'll give Dr. Morgan's office a call and see if I can run him over there for a check-up." Hymie Morgan was Arlene's veterinarian for her dog, Jet.

Arlene jumped as the bell on the door jingled. "Here." Arlene thrust the pup at Peggy. "Hold him and I'll go get that."

Peggy's eyes widened as she caught the pup's landing against her chest and Arlene ran out into the store to greet their visitor.

"Good morning, Mavis." Arlene rushed to the counter, wiping her damp hands with a paper towel. "How are you?"

"Hey, Arlene. I'm doing fine. I just stopped by to look for some duck cloth. I'm just needing about a yard or so."

"Are you looking for a particular color?" Arlene walked over to the wall where the cotton fabric bolts were standing in a color coordinated row. "What are you making?"

"Ah, I'm making an egg apron!"

Arlene's eyebrows shot up. "I didn't know you had chickens!"

"It's in the works! Daniel is putting up some fencing for me tomorrow if the rain stops. I got a few hens from Eli Buford and I'll be getting some baby chicks in a few weeks."

"How wonderful! I hope you plan to share all those fresh eggs." Arlene pointed to the top row. "The solid duck canvas is on the top left. There are a few prints there, too. We haven't put out all the spring fabric yet."

"I already have some cotton for the front,

but I need something sturdy for the back. I don't want it to be too flimsy." Mavis stroked her hand across the bolts. "Maybe a green or sienna? The printed fabric is green leaves on a beige background. I'll need some bias tape to match, too."

"Let me grab the step stool so I can pull these bolts down." Arlene walked into the storage room and found Peggy standing just where she left her. "Mavis Bell needs some duck cloth, so I need—. Where is the puppy?"

"Oh, he's running around here somewhere," Peggy huffed. "Probably peeing on everything."

Arlene scooped up the chubby furball and grabbed the step ladder with the other hand.

"I'll take care of Mavis. You take care of that." Peggy pointed to the pup as she took the folded step stool from Arlene.

"Hey, Mavis. Which bolt do you need?" Peggy popped the folded steps out and planted the stool near the fabric shelves as Arlene pulled her phone from her pocket to call Dr. Morgan's office.

"I brought a swatch of the cotton with me. Let me see the medium and the dark green." Mavis pointed. "I think the browns are darker than what I want, and beige will show dirt too easily."

Peggy carried the bolts to the cutting table. "Are you in the market for a dog?" Peggy grinned mischievously. "Arlene has a puppy that needs a home."

Mavis tilted her head. "No, not really, but..."

Slipping her phone back in her pocket, Arlene walked out of the back room with the pup in a football hold. The shivering had stopped, and his head pivoted around the room drinking in all the new places he might need to sniff.

Mavis beamed. "What a cutie! What's his name?"

"He doesn't have a name yet." Arlene held him up and squinted her eyes. "What do you think he looks like?"

"A name?" Peggy shook her head. "He needs a home."

"He looks like an Archie to me." Mavis hummed. "Or maybe a Clyde."

"Really? I was thinking more along the lines of Butterball or Jolly." Arlene squeezed her shoulders up and let them drop. "He's so cute and chubby."

"He won't be that way long." Peggy scowled. "They grow up, you know, after they pee on everything and chew up all your shoes."

Arlene waved her hand at Peggy dismissively. "Ignore her. She's a cat person."

Peggy winced and flipped the bolt over on the table so Mavis could choose her color. She had lost her cat, Lolly, several years ago and had never been able to risk that loss again.

"I love them all, but I've got too many already. With all the new chickens coming, I don't think it's a good time for me to train a puppy right now." Mavis placed her swatch down on each of the fabric choices and pointed to the lighter green. "I'll take a yard of this."

"I just called Doc Morgan, and Lily said he's out of the office today on farm calls. She said she'd work us in tomorrow, though." Arlene handed the pup to Mavis when she reached out for him.

"The shelter will be open in about thirty minutes." Peggy folded the cut fabric and pinned a ticket to it.

"The shelter!" Mavis rubbed her cheek on the puppy's head. "That's no place for a baby like this. Can't you take him, Arlene?"

"I can't." Arlene shook her head. "Jet doesn't get along with other dogs. He's very friendly to people, but I wouldn't trust him with a puppy. I've tried to get him a playmate before, and it just doesn't work out."

"Well, he can't stay here." Peggy walked to the cash register as Mavis stacked some thread and binding on top of the fabric.

"Couldn't you keep him for one night?" Arlene's eyes were pleading. "I'm sure I can find him a permanent home. I just need a little time and he needs to be checked out by the vet."

"No!" Peggy leaned back in disbelief. "I don't know what to do with a dog!"

"There's nothing to it." Mavis shrugged. "Feed him and give him a warm place to sleep."

"He's got to go." Peggy's stare drilled into Arlene.

"How about I take him for a few hours." Mavis glanced at Peggy and then at Arlene. The tension was snapping in the air. "I'm headed home now, and I can keep an eye on him until Daniel gets off work. We've got to run some errands when he gets off, so I'll need to pass the pup back to you then, but it's too wet for me to work outside today anyway."

"That would be great, Mavis! Thank you."

Sheri Richey

# Chapter 2

Amanda Stotlar tapped her knuckles on the door frame of Cora Mae Bingham's office. "Mayor? Are you going out to lunch today?"

"I was going to walk downtown, but I haven't checked the weather. Has the rain stopped?"

"Yes, but it's not warm."

"Hmm, maybe I should just heat up the soup I have. You can go ahead to lunch now, if you like."

"I was planning to run out to Fletcher Farms and see if I can catch my dad out there. He's not answering his phone, but his office says he should be there."

"Is something wrong?" Cora pulled off her

reading glasses and gave Amanda her full attention.

"Well, Arlene Emery just called, and she wanted to know if he could help with a puppy she found. I can't bring him home. Gypsy would never tolerate that!" Amanda rolled her eyes. Gypsy was an accidental wedding gift from Grace Keslar last year and the large gray cat had become their feline child instantly.

"I understand completely. Marmalade would be appalled as well. She's not even accepted the fact that other cats exist in this world. It is only her." Cora slipped her glasses back on her nose as she reached for her phone. "A dog would be out of the question. Can Shelby Worth help?"

Amanda cringed. "She's hoping to keep him out of the shelter, if she can."

"I wonder if the Chief would like a playmate for Briscoe. I can call him." Cora tapped her phone display to call Conrad Harris.

"She's trying to find him a good home by tonight, because he has nowhere to go."

Cora Mae left him a brief message when the police chief didn't answer and stood up to look out her office window. "You can go ahead to lunch. I think I'll stay in."

Amanda nodded and reached for her jacket hanging by the door just as Cora's phone rang.

"Connie?" Cora asked him to call back in her message, but she had told him it wasn't urgent. "I was just calling to see if you wanted another dog." Laughing at his response, she motioned for Amanda to wait. "Let me put you on speaker. Amanda is looking for some help."

"I can't keep up with Briscoe!" Conrad's voice boomed through the phone speaker. "I've decided once the weather evens out, I'm going to break down and have my backyard fenced in. I know he needs exercise, but I'm too old to prance around town in the winter anymore."

Amanda stepped closer to the phone. "Arlene Emery found a puppy this morning that someone dumped in the alley. She's hoping to find someone to take him."

"Well, she could check in the station tonight when Officer Kimble comes on duty. She's pretty fond of Briscoe so I know she's a dog lover. Fred Rucker is working this weekend, and he could be another option."

"She really needs help tonight." Amanda moaned. "The little guy has nowhere to go. Arlene can't take him home. If you think of anyone who could take him this afternoon, can you ask them to call her down at the craft store?"

"I'll do that."

Cora Mae shrugged in defeat as a rhythmic beeping pierced her ears and she grabbed the phone to turn down the volume. "Are you outside?"

Amanda slipped her jacket on and whispered goodbye before leaving.

"Yeah, I'm down at Wade's garage. They're towing in a new car." Conrad chuckled. "There was a little accident out at Cajun Motors this morning."

"Where the deals are HOT!" Cora Mae

imitated the local commercial that played on the radio far too often.

"That's the place!"

"Was anyone hurt?"

"Nah, just a little misunderstanding. Marty Nash hit one of their cars and Ella Quinn is the one that's hot right now."

Cora Mae laughed at the vision of the tiny woman with the fiery personality, who strutted like a grazing chicken. Ella owned the used car lot west of town and people routinely underestimated her. Her diminutive frame could pack a punch and had actually done so a few times. "Was he test driving a car?"

"No, he's working there now." Conrad cleared his throat. "Or at least he was this morning. I don't know how this might affect his future employment status."

"Oh, my," Cora giggled. "That's unfortunate."

"I followed the car down here to escape the screaming tirade that was happening at Cajun Motors. I don't need to watch the car tow.

Have you had lunch?"

"I haven't, but I let Amanda go to lunch early. She's trying to reach Hymie to see if he has an answer for that dog. Do you want to go with me tonight to the play rehearsal? We can get dinner first."

"That sounds like a plan."

---

"I can't take this racket! What is that man doing over there?" Peggy growled as she broke down the box she had emptied. A new merchant had moved next door into the tiny space she had hoped to buy but had been unable to finance.

"I'm sure there's a lot to do over there to get ready to open. Do you remember when you opened the craft corner?" Arlene was seated behind the counter sorting through cross stitch kits.

"Yeah, I know. It's hard work, but I still don't like listening to it."

"Have you met him yet?" Arlene glanced up. "Cora Mae told me he's opening a barber shop! Won't that be nice? We haven't had one in years and unless the guys want to go to Paxton, they have to go to a beauty shop. Hobart would never do that."

Peggy shrugged.

Arlene husband, Hobart Emery, had passed away last year, and she was finally able to talk about him without reliving it. "He said a rooster didn't belong in a hen house." Arlene chuckled. "He wouldn't have been comfortable in Louise's beauty shop."

Peggy ripped open another box. "I don't know him."

"He's a young man. I saw him the other day."

"Yeah, I saw him, too." Peggy chuckled. "He has handlebars for ears! I was too shocked to speak to him."

Arlene shook her head in disapproval. "We should introduce ourselves. Be neighborly."

"Go ahead," Peggy said flippantly. "Go see if *he* needs a dog." Arlene had spent half the day on the phone calling everyone in town about that silly pup already.

Arlene's index finger popped up in the air. "Good idea! Why didn't I think of that?"

Peggy muttered and shook her head. "I don't know, but you need to figure that out soon. As soon as I'm done here, I need to run over to the community center for the play rehearsal. Eleanor said she needs to talk to me about the costumes for the play. Can you lock up tonight?"

"Sure. I'll be right back." Arlene tossed the sewing kits in her lap up onto the counter and grabbed her coat. "I'll tell him you said hello."

Peggy smiled at Arlene's demure scolding. Someone had to be the nice guy and she wasn't trained for that. The last year had been a challenge. She wanted Arlene around but paying for her help had really set her back. When Hobart died and Arlene was lost in her thoughts, working part-time seemed the perfect answer for both of them. Peggy was tired of carrying the load alone. The holiday season this last year had not been as profitable as expected and her worries about the future of her store had resurfaced with a vengeance. It was a challenge to find the optimism necessary to get out of bed in the mornings.

Spinning around when the door chime jingled, Peggy saw Mavis with the wrinkled confused puppy under her arm. "Here." Holding the dog out to Peggy, Mavis looked over her shoulder. "There wasn't any open parking on Fennel Street, so Daniel is blocking traffic. I've got to go."

"Wait, uh—.

"Sorry. Tell Arlene to give me a call if I can help again."

Peggy caught the puppy like a hot potato and frowned down at the wistful face startled by the jingling door. "You again." Peggy pinched the furry flesh around the puppy's neck. "Are you going to grow into all this skin?"

Panting, the pup's tongue whipped out for a quick lick before Peggy could pull her face away.

"Why does everyone keep tossing you at me and running away? If I were you, I'd start to get a complex." Chuckling at her own quip, Peggy lowered her face to the smashed snout and let the puppy lick her nose. The puppy's breath was intoxicating, and Peggy quickly jerked back before placing him carefully on the floor. "Don't eat, pee, or pilfer anything. I've got to clear out these boxes."

When the door chimed again, the puppy squeaked like rubber soled shoes on a wet floor and Peggy saw Amanda Stotlar's sheepish smile. "Aw, how adorable!" Amanda squatted down to the puppy's level and let it lick her whole face. "You're just a little bruiser, aren't you? Does he have a name yet?"

"I don't think so." Peggy shrugged.

"He looks like a Buster to me. What do you think?"

"I'm leaning toward Walrus." Peggy

shuddered.

"You can call him Wally!"

"No, I'm not calling him anything. He's Arlene's problem."

"Is Arlene still here?"

"Yes. She's just next door, but she should be back in a minute. Can you watch the little runt while I take these boxes to the dumpster out back? I'm sure Arlene will be right in."

"Sure!"

"Oh, there she is." Peggy pointed at the door as she gathered up the paper debris from the floor.

"Sorry. I was chatting up the new neighbor. I see the fur-boy is back!"

"Yes, he's adorable," Amanda cooed as Peggy slid the flattened boxes toward the storeroom. "I just stopped in to let you know that my dad didn't have any luck finding him a place tonight. You could board him at the clinic, but there isn't anyone there at night."

"I hate to leave him alone." Arlene stroked the velvety ear.

"Chief Harris mentioned that there were a couple of officers down at the police station that might be interested in a puppy, but they work the night shift. I'll go down there with you, if you like. I think it's better to show up with the puppy than to call. It's much harder to say no to him if he's licking you in the face."

Arlene laughed. "That's a good idea, but I'm closing tonight, so I can't leave right now."

"Well, I'll take him down there. If I don't have any luck, I'll bring him back."

Arlene nodded and scratched the top of his head. "Okay. I'm here until six o'clock."

# Chapter 3

Peggy flipped down a chair seat in the auditorium and slumped down to wait for Eleanor Cline. She planned to rest her eyes for a few minutes until the scene ended. This day had been too long, and she just wanted to get home. Working on these play costumes had always been fun for her, but maybe it was time to let someone else take responsibility for this.

"Hi, Peggy." Cora Mae slipped into the seat beside her and leaned her shoulder close to lower her voice. "What do you think about this new play, Murder is in the Heir?"

Peggy sighed and straightened up in her chair. "I haven't really paid any attention to it.

I've popped in a couple of times but I'm only here for a few minutes, so I haven't seen much of it. I've never heard of it before. Is it any good?"

"This is my first visit, but it looks really cute. It's a play about a play and it's a comedy. What I've seen so far is hilarious. Eleanor told me that the audience gets to participate. I don't know how that's going to work." Cora Mae rolled her eyes. "She's keeping those details secret."

"Secret? Well, we can't have that! You are going to find out, aren't you?" Peggy chuckled. Cora did not like secrets kept from her. Everyone knew that.

"The Chief says he's going to find out, but I don't know if I can get it out of him. He thinks it's funny to keep things from me." Cora huffed. "I need some leverage."

Peggy hummed. "I'll give it some thought. Maybe blackmail? Or we could gang up on him?"

Cora Mae snickered. "I'm open to ideas."

Peggy rested her head against the back of the chair and smiled at the teasing. Cora's spunk should have been energizing, but Peggy could not muster more than a smile.

"How are you doing?" Cora patted Peggy's arm. "You look tired."

Peggy nodded. "I am. It's been a long day."

"We all have those." Cora tossed a worried glance her way. "You need to take care of yourself. You need to take some time just for you. We all neglect ourselves sometimes, but it catches up with us, you know."

"Yeah, but time off does not fit into my schedule right now. It's on my to-do list though." Peggy smiled and patted Cora's hand. "Don't worry about me. I'll be fine."

"I do, though. We need to be there for each other. If you ever need help, I hope you know you can come to me for anything."

Peggy nodded as Eleanor Cline approached them with a long blue dress covered in clear plastic draped over her arm.

"Hi there, ladies. What do you think so far?" Eleanor glanced at the stage.

"It's really cute. I think everyone will love it." Cora winked.

"Well, I've got a dress for you." Eleanor tapped Peggy on the knee. "I was going to run it by the store today, but I just didn't get a chance." Eleanor slung it over the back of the chair in front of Peggy. "Nina brought it in last night and she thought it would work well for her part. She's playing Fiona Starkweather, who is the billionaire's niece. She said it's too big, but maybe that's all the work it needs, if you could just take it in a bit. It looks pretty old, but…" Eleanor shrugged. "Fingers crossed."

Peggy nodded. "I'll see what I can do. She'll need to come by the shop so I can measure. Tell her to drop in when she has a chance sometime this week."

"Will do! Thank you, Peggy." Eleanor hurried up the aisle and Peggy lifted the plastic to touch the fabric.

"This looks familiar." Peggy's forehead

creased and she pushed the plastic up higher. "This looks like a dress I made years ago for a high school play."

"Really?" Cora touched the blue tulle on the bodice.

"Olive. Do you remember when Olive Vogel was the drama teacher out at the high school? I made a dress like this for some play... I don't remember the name of it." Flipping the bottom of the dress up, Peggy looked at the side seaming near the waist. "This is my dress!"

"You made this? Are you sure?"

"Yes! Look, there's my tag. I always sew it into the side seams. I made this dress... I don't know, when did Olive die? Do you remember?"

"Twenty years ago." Cora looked up, straining her memory. "Maybe more. Where in the world has this dress been all that time?"

"I can't imagine. I'm going to ask the young lady where she got it when she comes in for a fitting. What was her name again?"

"Nina. That's all Eleanor said. I don't think I know anyone by that name, but she said she's playing the niece, so she should be here." Cora Mae pointed to the stage and squinted. "It could be the girl in the red shirt on stage next to Saucy right now, or it could be the young blond girl standing near Eleanor. Both of them are unfamiliar to me."

"Maybe Eleanor knows where Olive's costumes went after she died. She used to have a collection at the high school. I'll ask her about it. Maybe they are still there."

"Oh no! I wouldn't do that." Cora Mae shook her head. "There was a heated rivalry between those two back in the day. Eleanor hated Olive and was mad when Olive was chosen as the drama director. Eleanor thought it should have been her. She had seniority at the school and was quite angry about it at the time. I wouldn't open that can of worms if I were you."

"Surely that wound has healed by now. Olive's been dead for years!"

Cora smirked. "Perhaps, but Eleanor seems the type to hold a grudge to me."

Peggy frowned. Cora Mae was right. It could be risky. "I'll see what I can find out from the girl then." Peggy stood and draped the dress over her arm.

"Let me know what you find out," Cora waved at Conrad when she saw him scanning the seats looking for her. "You know I love a good mystery."

Peggy laughed as she turned to walk up the aisle.

"Are you ready to go?" Conrad slipped his arm in his coat. "Briscoe is ready to be picked up."

Cora Mae snickered. "Does he have his own cell phone now? Did he send you a text?"

His police dog, Briscoe, was certainly smart enough to handle that. "No. He told Sam to call me instead." Conrad laughed.

"Has he had dinner?" Cora Mae waved to her friend, Saucy, as they left the auditorium.

"Oh, yeah. I fed him before I left the station. Sammy just said he's pacing around the station from room to room. He was worried that maybe he needed to go outside."

"Poor boy, maybe we need to stop there first before you take me home."

"Nah, I think he's just looking for me. He'll be fine." Conrad opened the car door for Cora. "Sammy said Amanda dropped by with that puppy she's trying to home, and that's probably caused a stir down there. Sammy told her he'd watch him for the night because they haven't found him a place yet."

"Is Briscoe okay with other dogs?" Cora Mae grimaced. "He wouldn't hurt the pup, would he?"

"Nah, Briscoe usually doesn't engage with other dogs at all. If the puppy was trying to play with him, he might be pacing around to get away from it." Conrad chuckled. "His old girlfriend from the shelter, Doozie, was the exception. They had a shared past, I guess. Otherwise, I've always found him to shy away from any dog meet and greets."

"It's actually Arlene Emery who found the puppy and Amanda was trying to help her.

Neither of them could take him home, but I'm sure he'll find his person."

Conrad nodded. "I was surprised to see Saucy is doing another play. Did you know he was going to be there tonight? He always says he's not doing another."

Cora Mae laughed as she slid into the car and waited for Conrad to climb in the driver's seat. "He just says that when he's nervous about his lines. He has theater in his blood."

"He can be a bit theatrical."

Cora Mae smiled. Harvey Salzman, who everyone called Saucy, was a wiry senior citizen who had more energy than a kindergarten class on the last day of school.

"Is Peggy doing all right?" Conrad glanced over at Cora when she didn't answer right away.

"She seems a bit rundown. I think she's working too hard."

"That's always been her way."

"I think she's tired, but she'll never admit it. Peggy always says everything is fine, but I can see exhaustion and worry in her eyes. I just wish she'd let someone help her once in a while."

"I thought adding Arlene in at the store would do that." Conrad pulled into the parking lot of City Hall where Cora's car was parked.

"I'm not sure she could really afford to do that. That may have created a burden. I know Dorothy told me that everyone in the merchant's association has been grumbling about what a tough year they've had. The holiday season wasn't what they expected. I wish I could think of something more to do for them. We need to bring shoppers to Spicetown!"

Conrad nodded. "Good luck with that. Times are hard for everybody right now."

"Peggy did have a little surprise fall into her lap tonight though." Cora turned in her seat when Conrad parked beside her car. "Eleanor brought her a costume that needs to be altered for one of the cast members, and it turned out to be a dress that Peggy made for a high school play over twenty years ago!"

"She remembers it?" Conrad frowned.

"Her name is in it! Before Eleanor was drama director, there was a teacher named Olive Vogel who directed all the high school plays. Peggy made the dress for Olive."

"Wow, I wonder where it's been all these years."

"No idea. Olive died back when I was still teaching school, so I don't know where all of those old costumes went after that. They must not have been left at the high school. Eleanor said one of the girls in the play brought it to her last night."

"Interesting."

"Peggy is going to ask the girl about it when she does the fitting."

"The family probably kept some of her stuff thinking someone might need it someday."

Cora nodded. "Maybe. I can't wait to hear what she finds out."

Conrad chuckled as Cora opened the car door.

"You know I love a good mystery!"

Sheri Richey

# Chapter 4

Parking next to the side door of the police station the next morning, Conrad clipped the leash to Briscoe's harness before opening his door. Another gloomy, cool spring day stretched out across Spicetown, leaving everyone puzzled when the sun would warm things up and put winter behind them.

Briscoe led the way in when Conrad opened the door and before it shut behind him, he heard a squawking sound from the dispatch cubicle and then saw a fat, stubby pup bound down the hallway, headed straight for them both. Briscoe stiffened and Conrad dropped the leash to catch the running furball as Briscoe slipped into Conrad's office to avoid the collision. The pup had both legs out in front of him to stop, but slid on his belly, right into Conrad's feet.

Briscoe peered out at Conrad from his dog bed, uninterested in greeting the pup, so Conrad carried him back to the dispatch room. "Look what I got."

Georgia Marks, the dispatcher for the day, turned in her chair. "I know, Chief. Isn't he adorable?"

"Yeah, I guess, but what's he doing here?"

"Arlene is coming to pick him up. She should be here any minute. I hear he's pretty fond of Briscoe. Don't you think Briscoe could use a buddy?"

"I don't think the feeling is mutual." Conrad handed the puppy to Georgia.

"You could train him like Briscoe, and we'd have two police dogs!"

"It looks like someone smashed his sniffer." Conrad tapped the puppy's short snout. "I don't think he'd be much of a tracker with that nose."

Georgia scowled. "Maybe not, but he's awfully cute."

"He's got all that skin to grow into and he doesn't even know how to bark right." Conrad chuckled. "He can sure lick a face good and proper though."

"I'm so sorry I'm late." Arlene bustled through the lobby doors waving her hand at Georgia. "I was on the phone with a friend too long. I'm still trying to find this little guy his forever home. I hope he wasn't any trouble."

"Oh no, the little crouton is doing just fine. Sam named him Crouton." Georgia rolled her eyes. "I know he enjoyed having him around last night. I'm just sorry no one could keep him. Most of us work ten-hour shifts and it's just too hard to manage pets at home when you're away for so many hours."

"I understand." Arlene reached out to take the puppy. "I'm going to take him to see Dr. Morgan this morning and have him checked out. I'm hoping Hymie has some ideas for me.

Thank you all so much. You don't know how much I appreciate it. Have a wonderful day!"

"You, too!" Georgia waved as Arlene rushed out the door with the little bundle under her arm.

"I need coffee." Conrad nodded before turning to walk toward the break room.

"Ella Quinn called for you already." Georgia looked over her shoulder to see if that slowed Conrad's departure.

"Did you tell her we'd file the report with the county for her?"

"I did, but she needs the report number so she can file an insurance claim."

"She can call the county in a day or two!" Conrad threw up his arms as he walked through the break room door. *I try to help these people out by taking a report that is outside my jurisdiction and they still want something more.*

"She's in the parking lot, Chief." Georgia yelled out when she saw Ella Quinn get out of her car on the camera monitor. She held her hand on her head to keep her cowboy hat on and shoved the car door shut with her hip. A magnetic sign on the car door edged in flames, showed a long red pepper curled into a "C" spelling out 'Cajun Motors - Where all the deals are HOT!'

Conrad closed his eyes in a brief meditation before filling his pitcher with water.

"Morning, honey!" Ella rubbed the cold from her arms as she approached Georgia's counter. "Is the Chief in?"

Conrad stopped in the doorway with his water pitcher in his hand. "Morning, Ella."

"Oh, I'm so glad I caught you! I just need an itty bitty minute of your time, if that's okay." Her southern drawl oozed out, coated in sugar when she wanted something.

"Come on back."

Briscoe stayed in his dog bed with a watchful eye as Ella followed Conrad into his office. Removing the top of his coffee maker, he poured the water in and spoke over his shoulder. "What can I do for you today?"

Ella removed her hat and fluffed her hair. "I'm needing that report number, Chief. I've got to file my claims right away. That silly boy has cost me a ton of money. I've got two cars damaged, and Wade ain't fixin' them for free."

"Ella, now I explained all that to you yesterday. You're in the county, so all I did was gather the info. I'll send it to the county, and you'll need to get your report from them."

"But you have to write it up to send it there. I'm sure that will be good enough. I just need a copy of that and then I'll run it over to the insurance man. I bet he'll take it from you."

"I don't have anything to give you, Ella. I'm sorry, but you'll have to wait a day or two."

Ella pouted. "I need those cars fixed, Chief."

"What about Marty Nash? Aren't you going to make him pay for it?" Conrad turned to go to his desk and took a step back when he saw Ella standing right behind him. She had high-heeled boots on that made her almost a normal height, but the pink western outfit decorated with silver medallions and fringe was a bit distracting. She never blended into a room.

"I don't know what to do with that boy! I started to fire him on the spot, but then I told him he had to work it off. He doesn't have two pennies to rub together. I knew he couldn't pay for the repairs."

"Did he give you any explanation?" Conrad sat down at his desk and motioned for Ella to take a chair across from him.

"He said just as he turned to pull the car into the parking spot, the sun blinded him, and he clipped the car next to it." Ella smirked. "I think he's got a problem that sunglasses can't cure."

"What do you mean?"

"I know he drinks too much. I've smelled it on him, and it's that day old seeping out of your pores kind of alcohol from drowning in it the night before. You know what I mean?"

Conrad nodded.

"Dwight says the boy has been messed up

since his mama died. He never quite got over it."

"Dwight?"

"Yeah, Dwight Jackson. He works for me cleaning up the cars and what not."

"When did Marty's mother die?" Conrad leaned forward in his chair and the creaking woke Briscoe.

"Oh, years ago. He was just a kid, Dwight said. Dwight grew up with Marty's mama. You know, he's been around since God was a boy. He knows everybody."

"I didn't realize Marty was a Spicetown native. I thought he was new to town. I'd never met him before."

"Oh, he left as a young'un. Went in the service for a while but he's been moved back here to town for a couple of years. He was working down at Wade's before I hired him."

"Maybe he could fix the cars himself then." Conrad held his hands out in offering. "If he worked at Wade's Garage, he has to know something about it."

Ella hummed. "You might have something there. Maybe Wade will take some green off the price if I trade Marty out to him for the job." Ella smiled. "That's awful clever of you, Chief. I'm gonna go down there and see if I can't cut me a deal!" Ella jumped out of her chair and Briscoe tensed.

Conrad chuckled. "I hope you can get that to work for you."

"Well, you know that's my specialty. I do know how to make a deal!"

Ella's footsteps clicked down the hallway as Conrad got up to pour his fresh coffee and send up a silent prayer for those at Wade's Garage that were completely unaware of what was headed their way.

---

Arlene opened the door of the Spicetown Animal Clinic and looked around at the empty waiting room. She had hoped to sneak in early before the morning appointments started.

"Oh, Ms. Emery, what do you have there?" Lily Tanner reached out both hands to scratch behind the puppy's ears as Arlene held him up to peer over the counter.

"Someone dumped this poor baby in the alley behind the Carom Seed Craft Corner and we found him yesterday. I need to get him checked out, and I was hoping you might know if someone was looking for him. He really needs a good home. I just can't keep him."

"We haven't gotten any lost puppy reports, but Doc might know someone interested. Let me go ask him."

Arlene paced around the lobby waiting until Hymie Morgan appeared.

"Morning, Arlene. Whatcha got here?"

Arlene held the squirming puppy up in the air and Hymie lifted up his ear flaps for a glance. Slipping his finger in the side of his mouth, he tried to look at his teeth, but the pup wanted to gnaw on his finger instead. "Amanda told me you found him downtown. I'm sorry I was out of pocket yesterday, but this guy looks pretty healthy." Hymie took him from Arlene and felt his belly and hips. "He's a chubby little biscuit, but he's old enough for shots and worming. Do you want to leave him up here with us today?"

Arlene's eye brightened. "Could I? Yes, that would be great!"

"We'll work him in today and keep him out front in the exercise pen. Maybe someone will be interested in giving him a home."

Arlene put a hand over her heart. "Oh, that would be wonderful."

"Come back by this afternoon before five o'clock and we'll have him ready to go for you."

Arlene nodded as Hymie handed the puppy to Lily.

"Does he have a name?" Lily let the pup lick her cheek.

Arlene shook her head. "No, not yet."

"Well, today his name is Biscuit!"

Sheri Richey

# Chapter 5

Peggy entered the store from the alley and walked to the front to flip on the heat and lights. The mornings were still too chilly, and the empty store was bone cold in the mornings. Dragging out her box of stickers from behind the counter, she stared at the fabric bolts on display and counted how many were seasonal patterns. She needed to tag the ones to remove and replace with spring colors before beginning to swap them out.

After stewing about it all evening, Peggy had decided she would need to cut Arlene's hours. There was no other way to make ends meet. Crafting sales always decreased after the winter holidays. Many of the fiber crafts were only popular in the colder months, and much of her income came from yarn sales, which would shrink through the summer. She hated to do it. She needed Arlene's help, and she thought Arlene needed to be needed, but her grand idea of opening a shipping store in the adjacent space had been dashed.

The space now occupied by the new barber had been vacant for over two years since the ice cream shop closed. Vicki Garwin, owner of the Fennel Street Bakery, had now begun carrying a few flavors of ice cream and the space was too small for most shop owners. Peggy had hoped she could open a doorway between the two business fronts and handle package shipments for the town. With all the online ordering, the demand had increased and Spicetown residents had to drive to Paxton to ship or return packages. She thought she had an excellent business plan to support her idea, but the bank had not agreed.

Remembering the costume she had hung up beside her coat in the back room, she dropped the sticker box and decided to take a closer look at the dress first. Returning with the adjustable dress form rolling behind her, she wanted to check for fabric damage. The edges of the beige ruffling had yellowed and there was a small tear in the back that she could fix. The dress didn't smell musty at all, so it must not have been in storage.

Before Peggy could toss the dress over the dress form, she heard a tapping on the glass door and saw a young woman with stringy brown hair waving at her. Motioning her to come in, she tossed the dress on the knitters' couch in the back of the store.

"Sorry, are you open?"

"Yes, come in. I just forgot to turn the sign over. My mistake." Peggy reached over and flipped the closed to open.

"I'm Nina Arnett. I'm in the play, and Eleanor Cline told me to come by. She said she gave you my dress."

"Oh, yes! It's right over here." Peggy walked to the back of the store, expecting Nina to follow. “We’ll have more room back here by the couch. I have a little group of knitters and crocheters that gather on Tuesdays. Do you do any crafting, Nina?”

“No. I wish I did, but I’m all thumbs. I don’t know how to do any of that stuff. My mother used to sew a little, but she never taught me.”

“Well, we have classes for any kind of craft you can imagine and special events at the community center regularly. Do you live here in Spicetown?”

“No, but I’m not too far.” Nina pointed west. “What do you think of the dress? Is it going to work okay? My sister gave it to me, and it just seems perfect for the part.”

“I think we can make it work. How long do you want it? Show me where you want it to hit and let’s start with that measurement.”

Nina held the side of her hand against her knee. “I think just below here. I’m playing an older lady, so I think it should be longer that what I’d wear.”

"That's a safe length. You don't want to trip on it, and you don't want it to fly up in case you trip and fall." Peggy smiled when she saw worry creep across Nina's face. "Don't worry. I'm sure that won't happen. Have you been on stage before?"

"Just in high school. I played Wendy in Peter Pan, and everybody said I was really good. I've got a good memory, and I can project my voice really far." Nina's high pitched squeaky voice would have been well received in the role of a children's character.

"The community center here has individual microphones that you'll wear, so you won't have to speak too loudly." Peggy turned Nina around by her shoulders and measured her waist.

"Cool!"

Peggy wasn't certain voice projection was the best quality to have when you spoke like Mickey Mouse. "Where did your sister get this dress? Has she had it a long time?"

"She didn't say, but I don't think so. I

think she got it at the resale shop in Red River. She goes in there all the time. Have you ever been there?" Nina held her arms out so Peggy could wrap the measuring tape around her.

"I've been to Red River, but I didn't know they had a resale shop." Peggy patted Nina on the shoulder to let her know she could relax her arms.

"Yep, it's called HERS. It stands for high-end resale shop. Isn't that cute? My sister went to school with the lady that opened it. It's not been there very long, but there are lots of clothes and other stuff like shoes and jewelry."

"Okay, I'm all done. I'll get it cleaned after I alter it and we'll do a fitting before show night. Okay?"

The door jingled as Arlene walked in and removed her coat.

"Give me your phone number and I'll text you when it's ready." Peggy handed her notepad to Nina to write her number.

"Great! Thank you so much! I'll see you later." Nina hurried out the front door and

Arlene's eyebrows went up.

"Was that a new cast member?" Arlene hung her coat up and walked over to the sofa to see the dress.

"Yes, her name is Nina, and she said her sister gave her the dress." Peggy lifted the skirt and pulled out the tag for Arlene to see.

"Oh, wow! You made this dress?"

"Yeah, I thought it looked familiar when Eleanor gave it to me last night, but I wasn't certain until I looked for my tag. I made this twenty years ago! I was floored."

"Where in the world did she get it?"

"She said her sister gave it to her, but she thinks she got it from a secondhand store in Red River. I'm going to call them and see if they have other costumes. If they do, I'm going over there." Peggy slipped the dress on the mannequin and measured from the waist down to put a straight pin for the hemline.

"You think they might have more of your dresses? Who did you make this for?"

"Olive Vogel. Did you know her? She was

the drama teacher years ago, and this dress was made for a high school play."

Arlene shook her head. "No, but I knew who she was. She must have had a lot of costumes. Do you think they all might be over there?"

"It's worth a shot. I know the community center could use them if they are there, and I guess it's crazy, but I'm feeling kind of possessive about them." Peggy blushed. "I know it's silly, but they have a piece of me, and I don't want them being sold off for pennies to strangers."

Arlene laughed. "They are like your children!" It was the closest thing either of them had to offspring. "I feel the same way about my quilts. I am happy to gift them to people I know, but I need to feel like they are taken care of and appreciated. A lot of work goes into our projects. People who don't craft, just don't get it."

"Exactly!"

"Vogel? Wait, that's the name of the guy

next door." Arlene pointed to the wall that separated the craft shop from the planned barber shop. "Doug Vogel. Do you think he's related to Olive?"

"What? Really! I didn't know that. Olive had children. Could that be her son? It's not a common name. Cora Mae will know. I told her I'd let her know when I found out where the dress came from, so I'll ask her then. You know, she knows everyone who grew up here. If he went to Peppermint Elementary, Cora would know something about them."

"Has Olive Vogel passed away?"

"Oh yeah, years ago. Geeze, I can't even remember when it was. She was such a sweet lady, and she had so much enthusiasm for life."

"What happened?" Arlene sat down on the couch.

"A car accident. She hit the overpass out on Rosemary Road late one night. The weather was bad, and no one really knew the details. It was tragic."

"How sad," Arlene wrung her hands in her

lap.

"This dress should have been at the high school back in the drama department. I don't know what happened to her things after she passed."

Arlene jumped up from the sofa. "What's the name of the thrift shop? We should give them a call." Arlene opened the laptop on the front counter and clicked to open a search page.

"I can't remember. She told me." Peggy scowled. She should have written it down. "It's in Red River and I think she said it was a resale place. It may be new and not online yet."

"Found it! HERS, High End Resale Shop. It's open today. Do you want me to call?" Arlene pulled her phone from her sweater pocket and looked at Peggy.

"Yeah, go ahead."

Arlene tapped the number into her phone and handed it to Peggy.

"Hi, I'm calling from Spicetown, and I hope you can help me. I'm looking for costumes, like for a school play or a costume party. Does your store happen to have anything like that?" Peggy looked at Arlene and rolled her eyes.

"Are you sure? Someone told me they thought you did. I didn't want to drive over if they were wrong, though, so I thought I'd call first."

Arlene frowned.

"Okay, thank you." Peggy handed the phone back to Arlene. "The girl said they've never had anything like that, just used clothing, regular clothing. I don't know if she even understood what I was talking about."

"Well, if that's a dead end, I don't know where else to turn. There's a thrift shop in Paxton." Arlene shrugged her shoulders. "I could call them."

"What about the guy next door?" Peggy looked at the shared wall. "Let's see if we can find him online."

Arlene went back to the laptop.

"And look up Olive. See when she died. It was winter after the year 2000. I remember there was a big party that year on New Year's Eve and Olive co-hosted it with another teacher. Do you remember all the Y2K scare that everyone was obsessed with?

"Oh, yes." Arlene waved her hand. "That was all so silly."

"Well, the high school held an 'End of the World' party in the school gym as a joke and I remember going. It was probably one of the last times I saw her. Half the town was there."

"How sad." Arlene turned back to the laptop and leaned forward to read the obituary she found while a paper copy was printing behind her. "She was only 36 years old!"

"I know. She was young. If I recall, it was a bit of a mystery, kind of a freak accident. Everyone was shocked."

Arlene handed the printed copy to Peggy. "She had two sons; Marty was 17 and Doug was 13."

Peggy read the obit. "That guy next door is her youngest son."

"Yes, and that might explain how the dress

resurfaced. He told me he'd just moved back to Spicetown. His dad still lives here."

"His dad is Ralph Vogel, and he remarried right after Olive's death."

"The family must have had the costumes put away somewhere." Arlene ran her hand over the dress bodice. "This is really beautiful, Peggy. It's a shame it's been hidden away all these years."

"Thank you, and I think it's time we try to uncover all that we can find. Don't you? I know Olive would want them on stage again."

# Chapter 6

Cora Mae looked out the front window of the Caraway Cafe, watching for Conrad Harris. She had been a little early for lunch because she had decided to drive. The wind was still too chilly for her taste.

Peggy Cochran rushed in the door and headed straight for the order pickup counter without even seeing her.

"Peggy!" Cora wiggled her fingers in the air when Peggy turned around. After talking to Frank Parish over the counter, she took a seat across from Cora Mae.

"I was just going to call you after I picked up my lunch. I talked to that girl this morning about the dress."

"Oh!" Cora rubbed her hands together. "What did you find out?"

"She's clueless. She said she thought her sister bought it at a secondhand store in Red River, but we called them. No dice." Peggy leaned forward on her elbows and looked at Cora across the table. "I don't know what to do next. Arlene mentioned there was a thrift store in Paxton, but it sounds like this girl just doesn't know where her sister got the dress. I guess the mystery continues."

Peggy pulled the printed obituary from her pocket and unfolded it before handing it to Cora. "Arlene printed this for me."

Cora Mae read over the obituary as Dorothy Parrish approached their table with Peggy's carry-out lunch order. "Dorothy, did you know Olive Vogel?"

"Sure! Cute little gal that taught at Cinnamon High. Boy, that's been some years ago."

"Yes." Cora held up the printout. "She died in 2002."

Dorothy nodded. "Auto accident out on Rosemary Road. I remember."

"Tragic." Peggy took the lunches from Dorothy. "Apparently, one of her kids is opening a barbershop next door to me."

"Marty?" Dorothy leaned back in shock. "He can't be trusted with razors! That boy is not stable."

"Dorothy!" Cora Mae sat up straight in her chair. "Shhhh, why would you say something like that?"

"He's violent, Cora. He's got a problem and always has had. That's why he went into the service as a young boy. They were going to throw him out of school for fighting. Mean, I tell you! Now I hear he's drinking like his daddy did."

"Oh, I didn't know." Cora looked around the dining room and lowered her voice. "He was a quiet boy. I had him in school and he wasn't any trouble at all."

"He was a terror as a teenager." Dorothy propped her hand on her hip. "Olive was a sweet girl, but she sure had lousy taste in men."

"Who are you talking about? Is this the same guy next door to me?" Peggy leaned closer.

"No, Olive's oldest child is Marty Nash." Cora patted her hand. "The barber must be his younger brother."

"Oh, I saw that in the obituary. Vogel was her second husband." Peggy folded the printout Dorothy handed her and slipped it back in her pocket.

"Yeah, and he's an odd one, too." Dorothy rolled her eyes. "I don't think Olive had a minute of happiness there either, poor girl."

Cora Mae looked around again for eavesdroppers before speaking quietly. "I've heard, too. He wasn't very well liked. It is a shame."

"Well, Arlene's been over to meet the barber, but I haven't talked to him yet. I guess I need to test the waters."

The pickup bell on the counter rang and Dorothy held up her finger. "Gotta go, ladies."

"Me, too. Arlene's waiting on me." Peggy got up and pushed in her chair. "I think I'll do a little more digging on this issue, though. I'd like to find the rest of Olive's costume collection and learn a little more about that accident."

"I can ask the Chief if there's a file in his office on it. He ought to be here soon."

"That would be great. I think I'll check with Daniel Wittig and see if he knows anything."

"The new principal at the high school? I didn't know you knew him."

"He's my neighbor. I've never contacted him at the school, but we talk all the time in the yard. He's an avid gardener, so he's outside puttering around all the time."

"Good idea! Let me know what you find out and I'll get back to you on the police file."

"Great! See you later, Cora."

When Peggy returned to the Carom Street Craft Corner, she found Arlene sitting on the knitters' sofa in the back with Mavis Bell. Leaving the lunch bag on the counter, she walked to the back of the store.

"Is it teatime ladies?" Peggy smiled in teasing, but regretted her words when Arlene jumped up from the sofa and Mavis looked startled. "I didn't mean to interrupt."

"No, no. It's okay. Mavis just came by for some more bias tape and we were chatting."

"I put a whole strip of it on backwards!" Mavis slapped her hands on her legs. "I'm getting senile in my old age."

Peggy laughed. "It's very easy to do. Did Arlene already ring you up?"

"Yeah, I've got it. I should be going. I'll give you a call, Arlene."

"Okay, Mavis. Take care."

"Lunch is on the counter." Peggy pointed and slipped her sweater off. Tossing it over the back of the sofa, she studied Arlene. "Is everything okay? Is Mavis all right? You both looked in shock when I came in the door."

"Oh, yes. It's nothing. Mavis just came by to make me a proposition." Arlene fluttered her eyelids and pretended to laugh, although there was concern etched across her forehead.

Peggy opened the lunch bag and pulled out the Styrofoam containers, handing one to Arlene. "What kind of proposition?"

"Thank you." Arlene took her lunch back to the sitting area at the rear of the store and avoided Peggy's eyes.

"You don't have to tell me. It's none of my business. I didn't mean to pry." Peggy handed Arlene a napkin, wondering if the offer involved a job of some sort. Perhaps this would be a good time for her to talk to Arlene about reducing her hours.

"Oh, no, it's not that. I'm just still trying to get my head around what she said." Sitting back and balancing her lunch on her lap, Arlene grabbed a potato chip and popped it into her mouth.

Peggy sat her lunch on the small coffee

table and opened condiment packages to load up her cheeseburger before cutting it in half, waiting for Arlene to continue.

"You know that property that Hobart used to farm? It's out North Road just across from Mavis' house."

"Yeah. You decided not to hire a new farm manager. Are you going to lease it or sell it?"

"I didn't want the headache of trying to keep it running, so I've just let it set. I was hoping to get an offer from someone wanting to lease it, but it's spring now and I haven't heard from anyone. I hadn't made a decision, but I almost feel like I need to sell it. It's not making me money anymore."

"Land is always an investment." Peggy shrugged. "It doesn't hurt to just hold on to it, unless you could make more money from another investment."

Arlene rubbed her hands over her face. "I hate all these financial decisions! This stuff makes me bonkers. I feel like whatever I decide, it will be wrong. It's like picking a checkout line. Whichever one I choose, it's the wrong one."

"But how does this involve Mavis?" Peggy covered her fries with ketchup. "Does she care what's across the street from her?"

"Mavis finally got her husband's life insurance from the coal mine. She put it in the bank initially, but now she thinks she wants to start her own hobby business with it."

"Hobby business?"

Arlene tilted her head. "She called it that. I think she means expanding her hobby to see if she can make some money from it. It will keep her busy and give her purpose. Mavis is technically retired, but she's working at Bryan's nursery all the time. She can't sit idle."

"Mavis wants to farm?" Peggy squinted her eyes and shook her head. "Is she wanting to lease your land?"

"No, she wants to buy it." Arlene stared at Peggy. "She has a business plan, and she wants to plant stuff, not crops, but trees and bushes. She said she'd build a greenhouse and use the barn for storage."

"She's going to compete against Bryan? I can't believe that. He's like another son to her!"

"No, she's going to supply him with what she grows. She'll be a plant distributor for him and other nurseries around the area. She's thinking about also planting part of the land in fruit trees, so she has fruit to sell at the farmer's market in a few years."

"Wow, that's a big undertaking! Does she remember how old she is?" Peggy laughed. They were all in their sixties and Peggy wanted to slow down, not start something new. "I'm exhausted just thinking about all that."

"I know. It made my head spin, too, but you know Mavis. She's full steam ahead all the time. She said her son, Danny, was really taking an interest in what she was doing, and she hoped the business would support him later. He can help her with the manual labor at first and then take over the business himself someday. Since Leann went back to St. Louis with the grandkids, I think she's really feeling alone. She's over at Bryan's even when she's not scheduled to work, just hanging out with him and his customers."

"She's filling that void with work." Peggy nodded. She knew many of her retired friends struggled with a loss of purpose when they no longer had a job forcing them out of bed each morning. Peggy knew she would never have that battle to fight. She had put aside all of her interests and hobbies for decades just to keep this business running. She was pining for the day she could relax without guilt and do whatever she wanted to do each day.

"Leasing land is a brilliant investment if you want a steady future income stream, but I don't really need that. I have no heirs for the land either, so selling and investing the money seems like the best idea."

"So, you're going to sell to Mavis?"

Arlene sighed. "I keep hearing Hobart's voice in my head saying 'never do business with friends'. That's my only reservation."

"It's a good thing Hobart isn't in *my* head!"

Peggy chuckled. "Or you wouldn't be sitting here!"

Arlene laughed and shook her head. "You're right. I'm glad, too!" She hadn't even hesitated to work for Peggy when she offered her this part-time job at the store.

Peggy cleaned up the table and threw away the sack. "I'm going to run over to the Spicetown Star, if you'll be okay alone for a while."

"Sure, it's quiet. Are you placing an ad in the paper?"

"No, I'm going to stop in and see what Sally knows about Olive's accident."

"Was she working there back then?"

"She's been there for thirty years, and she's got a mind like a sponge. She won't talk on the phone though because she thinks Ed listens in on her calls." Peggy laughed. "Knowing Ed, he probably does. That's why I always walk over there to place one."

"Did you see what he put in the paper Saturday? He is such a curmudgeon!" Arlene scowled. “I don’t know why I read that column of his. It’s always negative.”

“The Poisoned Pen?” Peggy chuckled. Ed Poindexter was the editor of the Spicetown Star newspaper, and he wrote a weekly column called The Pointed Pen, where he pointed his pen at something and usually tore it apart. “I always look at the title, just to make sure he’s not writing about me, and then I move on.”

“I wish I could do that. I don’t need any bad news in my world, but it’s like a car accident. I have to slow down and look at it,” Arlene huffed. “His last column was about recycling and how our city vendor is not adequate to meet the needs of the environment. “It’s a free service, for Pete’s sake! He listed all the things you can’t put curbside for pickup and then singled out hardback books to complain about. Who throws away books?” Arlene tossed her hands out. “Who would do that?”

Peggy laughed at Arlene’s bluster. “Settle down now. You can’t give in to him. He wants you to be frustrated and aggravated. Don’t let him win."

"What a despicable goal!"

"Indeed!" Peggy grabbed her sweater off the hook and slipped it on. "I'll be back in a few minutes."

# Chapter 7

Cora Mae scooted her chair closer to Conrad's desk as he turned his monitor around. After lunch, she had stopped by the police department so he could check the computer for Olive Vogel's accident report. Twenty years ago, the police department was just getting used to computer files and there was a paper file still maintained as a backup.

"That's a picture of the crash site." Conrad pointed to the concrete overpass. "She veered off to the side and hit the side abutment of the overpass, that concrete substructure that holds it up."

Cora Mae grimaced and looked away. "That's right after the Michaels' curve." Jim and Julie Michaels owned a large cattle farm in the area, and the farm entrance was right before a sharp curve in Rosemary Road, so everyone named it after them. "That's outside the Spicetown limits."

"Yeah, but from the report, Spicetown officers were first on scene. We were closer."

"Does the report say what they think caused the accident?"

"Speculation was icy patches on the road." Conrad turned the monitor back to its original position. "It had gotten above freezing that day but dropped down again below at night so some of the melting snow had frozen over. There's a low spot on the inside of that curve and it could have been slick there."

"She probably hit that patch in the middle of her turn." Cora Mae shuddered. "What time did this happen?"

"The call came in at 11:20pm from a Gregory Holtsby, who lives near Connor's Bluff. He saw it on the road and stopped to check on the driver. He didn't have a mobile phone, and he felt like he couldn't bang on any doors at that hour, so he couldn't call it in until he got home."

"That half hour might have saved her life."

"No, he said he checked on her and she was gone."

They sat in silence while Conrad read the rest of the report and Cora Mae settled her thoughts.

"Where in the world could she have been going at that time of night?" Cora frowned. "Her boys? Where were they? She lived on Long Pepper Lane."

"They were home, it says. The county put in a call to the state family services because they couldn't find the husband right away, though."

"Well, where in tarnation was Ralph?"

"It doesn't say." Conrad shrugged. "The county report might have more information. All I have is what they gathered at the scene."

"I know Greg Holtsby. He worked for the City back then. He retired right after Bing passed away and I became mayor. This must haunt him day and night. I know it would if I'd come up on it."

Conrad nodded. "Tell Peggy she can order the report online from the State if she's interested. They redact the names, but she can get a copy if she wants one. There might be different information in the county's initial report. I don't have a copy of that."

"I'll tell her. Did anyone take pictures of the road itself, the curve before the accident?"

"They did, but there's nothing there. It was hours after the accident, though, so no one can really say what was there at the time. Maybe it wasn't ice. Maybe she ran a tire off the blacktop edge and that made her lose control. It's not uncommon for sharp curves like that to cause accidents. That's why you always see crosses and flowers at those sites."

Cora Mae nodded. Olive would not have been familiar with that road living on the other side of town, and it was late at night. "Who was the reporting officer for the county?"

"Cantrell."

"Sergeant Cantrell?" Cora only knew a few

of the county deputies.

"Yes, but he wasn't a sergeant yet. Twenty years ago, he was just a night shift deputy."

"And he's probably handled a hundred accidents since then."

"Probably, but that doesn't mean he won't remember it. Most of the accidents we handle don't have people dead on the scene."

"Thank goodness for that!" Cora Mae stood up with wobbly knees and grabbed her purse. "I better get back to work now. Thank you for the information. I'll talk to you later."

---

"Sally," Peggy hissed and waved her hand to motion Sally back to her desk. She didn't want anyone else to see her, especially not Ed Poindexter.

"Hey, Peggy! How are you?"

"I'm good. Do you have a minute?" Peggy whispered.

Sally sat down behind her desk. “Sure, what’s up?”

“Do you remember Olive Vogel’s accident?”

Sally nodded her head. “Yes! Olive was such a sweet lady. She used to bring me the play programs and help write up the advertising when the high school had a production, then give me free tickets for the staff to attend. She said it was so they would give it an excellent review, but of course we would do that anyway. It’s Cinnamon High!”

Peggy smiled remembering her giddy personality. Drama was the perfect place for her. She couldn’t have been more different from Eleanor Cline. “I was wondering if you could pull up the articles about her accident. I’ll pay for the copies.”

Sally waved her hand dismissively. “No need for that.” Sally looked over her shoulder to see if Ed was watching and turned to type into her computer. “It looks like there were only two and the obituary.”

"I won't need the obit. I found it on the funeral home's website."

"Do you mind my asking why?" Sally scrunched up her shoulders with a quizzical look.

"Oh, just curious." Peggy relaxed and leaned on the counter. "Her youngest son is opening a business next door to mine, and I just wanted to refresh the details in my mind. It's been so long..."

"It has. 2002. It says here her kids were 13 and 17 then. How sad."

"Yes, and I don't know them at all. The young man seems very quiet and hasn't come over to my shop yet. I'll have to go over and meet him."

"Well, he hasn't been in town long and he hasn't come in yet for ads, but I heard he was opening a barber shop. I didn't realize it was next to you. The old ice cream shop?"

"Yes. He's over there working away, but I haven't heard when he plans to open."

"He moved away after high school and just

recently returned. I don't know where he's been, but I hear he's engaged to a young lady from Red River. I guess that's why he moved here."

"Where is Ralph?" Peggy had never met Ralph Vogel but remembered Dorothy's assessment. "Do you know him?"

"Yeah, I know him when I see him. He works in construction and has been on some job sites with my husband. We've run into him a few times and my husband stops and chats. He always ignores me and I'm glad of that."

"Your husband likes him?"

"Jerry is polite, and he's friendly to everybody, but I don't think he'd say they were friends. Jerry introduces me, and Ralph barely acknowledges that I'm standing there. It's happened more than once. The last time we saw him, I just walked off when he stopped to talk."

"I've heard he was not well liked."

"Yeah, Jerry said a lot of the other guys don't like him."

"They sound like an odd match. Olive was so outgoing. I guess opposites do attract."

Sally nodded. "I think she was over correcting her earlier mistake. Billy Nash was volatile, and Ralph was devoid of emotion. Neither were great guys."

"So, Ralph raised the boys?"

"I guess so, but I've never met the boys."

"Well, I'm about to. I hope the barber has some of his mother's personality in him, but this has been helpful. Thanks for the copies. I owe you!"

"You might want to check with the library for articles from the Paxton paper."

Peggy waved goodbye and escaped before Ed caught her chatting.

Walking back into the Carom Seed Craft Corner, Peggy saw Arlene pushing a rolling cart of fabric bolts from the back storage room. "I'm back!"

"Good! Did you get any new info?"

"I did! I saw Cora Mae and Dorothy at the

cafe earlier, too, so I need to get you caught up."

"I got all the winter fabrics in the back and these just need to be priced and put out now."

"I can do that tonight." Peggy patted a chair and sat back to tell Arlene all that she learned from the cafe and the newspaper office. Telling the story helped her to organize her thoughts, and she knew what she needed to do next.

"I'm going to talk to Danny Wittig tonight when I get home and see if he will look around the school for the old costumes. He's only been working here a couple of years, and he probably doesn't know anything about them."

"Tomorrow is my day off, but I can pop in for a while if you need to run out to the school. I've got to pick up the puppy at the vet before five o'clock today. He's spending the night at my neighbor Margo's house tonight, but then I guess I'm at a dead end. Shelby is out of town, and I don't want to take him to the shelter. I don't know what to do with him tomorrow."

"You can bring him with you." Peggy

rolled her eyes. “Maybe if you had a cage with some paper in the bottom it would help, as long as he doesn’t stink the place up.”

Arlene squealed and gave Peggy a hug. “Thank you so much. He’ll be good. I promise!”

Sheri Richey

# Chapter 8

"Good morning, Ms. Quinn." Conrad tipped his hat and looked around the lobby of Cajun Motors. He hadn't been inside the building before, and he was surprised by the darkness of the lobby. Ella Quinn was a splashy personality, but she had not extended that to the decor of her business. A broken-down couch, plastic chairs, old wood paneling on the walls and dim lighting gave the impression of stepping back into a pool hall circa 1970, not a used car dealership.

"Chief! I was going to call you today."

"I thought you might." Conrad found out the county hadn't sent the report to Ella, so he had them scan him a copy and email it over. "I heard you were still needing the report, so I thought I'd drop it by."

Ella was looking right past Conrad, and he looked over his shoulder. A young woman was in the car lot, peeking through the window of a small hatchback. "Oh, Chief. Let me run outside just a minute and give that girl a howdy. I'm the only one here right now. I'll be right back."

"That's all right. I don't mean to keep you." Ella had already left the building before he finished his sentence. Conrad placed the report squarely on the counter and planned to leave by the side door, counting himself fortunate for the distraction.

Walking across the lobby, he heard footsteps in the side hall. "Ms. Ella will be right with you!" An old gentleman carrying a cane in one hand and a small cup in the other held his finger in the air to stop Conrad.

"I just saw her. She's out on the lot." Conrad pointed.

"She's havin' to run the whole place herself

today. Run a man ragged just a' watchin' her!" The man chuckled and sat down in one of the plastic chairs and spit in the cup.

"I'm Conrad Harris. I was just dropping something off for her."

"Ah, the PO-leece chief. Good to meet you. I'm Dwight Jackson." Propping his cane on the chair next to him, he nodded.

"Nice to meet you, Mr. Jackson." Conrad touched the bill of his hat. "Has it been busy today?"

"Not too bad, but that girl is burning the candle at both ends. I'm not much help to her, but I try to keep the place picked up."

"Is Marty Nash still working here?"

Dwight chuckled and shook his head. "He's trying, but she's got him over at Wade's Garage today, fixing his latest mistake."

"Yeah, I know about the fender bender. She told me she was going to talk to Wade."

"I warned her about him." Dwight shook his index finger at Conrad. "I told the girl he couldn't catch a bird if it lit on his finger. He might prove a runner for her, but he's no salesman."

"You know Marty well?"

"Since he was just his mama's wish, and I know this is not the right place for him, but he's got to figure that out his own self."

"His mother's accident was tragic. It happened before I moved to town, but I've seen the reports. Everyone speaks very highly of his mother."

"Yes, indeed! She was a gem, a flower in a field of weeds. I hope someday the truth comes out about that night."

"What do you mean?" Conrad couldn't deny his curiosity. He hadn't mentioned anything to Cora Mae, but the report had seemed to be lacking in detail, which left his mind open to speculation. The road conditions just didn't support the result.

"I'd like to know where that husband of hers was!" Dwight punched the air. "Lots of questions and no answers."

Conrad looked up when he heard the front

door open.

"Come on in, honey. Dwight, can you get Miss Cindy a cold drink? We're going to talk a few numbers here." Ella pointed the young woman to a chair and grabbed a stack of forms from behind the counter.

Dwight grunted as he rose to his feet. "Duty calls."

"Oh, Chief. I'm so sorry I ran out on you."

"That's fine, Ms. Quinn. I was just chatting up Mr. Jackson. I left your paperwork on the counter. You both have a nice day now." Conrad pushed the side door open.

"Thank you, Chief. I appreciate you!"

---

Peggy was almost finished packing the winter merchandise and putting it in storage when she heard the door chimes jingle. Arlene elbowed her way through the door with a pup under one arm and dragging a flattened metal cage with the other hand that banged against the door.

"Let me help!" Peggy rushed to get the end of the cage and they walked it to the storage room. "This looks huge."

"Well, Buddy spent the night with my neighbor, Margo, last night, and she loaned me this cage. She uses it when her granddaughter's dog stays with her, and she's a much larger breed."

"Buddy?" Peggy smiled and cocked her head, assuming Arlene had given in and accepted the pup as part of her family now.

"Oh, that's just what Margo was calling him, her little buddy. He's had about six different names so far." Arlene laughed. "None of them seem to stick. I guess it's as hard to find a name as it is to find a home."

"It's only been a couple of days. Don't lose heart yet." Peggy stared down at the flat rectangle of black mesh and put her hands on her hips. "Do you know what to do to make it turn into a cage?"

Arlene winced. "Well, ... She showed me,

but—."

"Is there a magic word that makes it pop up?" Peggy laughed and squatted down for a closer look. Slowly, lifting the top layer, she saw it was connected to the next panel. "I think we need a map!"

Arlene struggled out of her jacket, still holding the pup, and leaned over to reach for the second panel. Pulling them both up created a perfect rectangle with both ends open. "I remember this now. It all sort of unfolds and comes up into a box."

"Well, there! That's a good start." Arlene stepped back to admire their progress just as Peggy released her hold of the panel and both of them screamed as the box collapsed with a thunderous clang.

Peggy had tried to jump back from her crouched position and fallen right back on her backside as they both dissolved into laughter when the puppy yipped in celebration of the chaos.

"That thing could take an arm off!" Peggy

rocked herself forward and crossed her legs as Arlene dabbed tears of laughter from the corner of her eyes.

"A bit like a Venus flytrap, isn't it?" Arlene put the puppy on the floor. "Don't run off. Let me hold it up."

Peggy reached up and pulled up the other side so they were back where they were before so they could study the situation. "The small ends are on the inside now. I wonder if we should turn it on its side."

They both pushed to turn it, just as the bottom tray fell forward on top of the next panels and Arlene jumped to keep her fingers from getting pinched, but Peggy righted the crate again. "Bad idea, I guess."

Arlene chuckled. "I don't remember Margo turning it. I think we reach inside and pull those ends out." Finally, sitting down on the floor and crossing her legs in front of her, she held the heavy, long sides upright as Peggy cautiously stuck her arm inside to lift the side panel.

"Don't let go! I feel like I'm putting my hand in an alligator's mouth." Weakened from laughter, Peggy stood the side panel up, but it wouldn't fit through the hole. "How do we get it on the outside?"

"Maybe I should call Margo."

"I think we're close. Watch your fingers!" Wrestling the panel almost straight, Peggy worked around the edges to force the panel out. As soon as it popped out, Peggy stood up and leaned over the box. "What makes it stay together? Are there clips or something?"

"No, Margo just popped it together."

"Wait, I see it. There are these little curvy things on the edge." Peggy fought with the panels to get them straight and hooked into the hooks on the edge. "This thing is a bit of a death trap, don't you think?"

Arlene reached around to the other side and pulled the end panel up, and Peggy came around to try to snap it together the same way. "What if we put the pup in there and it collapses on his head?"

Peggy paused and looked around. "Where is that dog?"

"Have you got this? I'll go look for him." Arlene looked around the storage room when Peggy nodded and waved her away. Three of the sides were standing and Peggy was struggling to get the last side to snap in.

Arlene hadn't paid attention to which direction he had wandered once she sat down on the floor to help and wasn't sure where to begin. Scanning the storage area, she only saw a small puddle around the corner, which she quickly cleaned up before Peggy could see it. Exhausting all the potential hiding places, she walked into the store and looked around each aisle. The store was silent. On the verge of panic, Arlene looked in the restroom, under the couch and on the bottom of every shelf.

"Got it!" Peggy called out to Arlene. "I don't know if we'll ever get it flattened out again. We may have to buy Margo a new one." Peggy laughed as Arlene walked up to inspect.

Pushing on the top, Arlene leaned her

weight into it and then shook it. It kept its shape. “You’re a wizard!” Arlene chuckled.

“Where’s the dog?”

Arlene bit her lip. “I can’t find him.”

“What do you mean, you can’t find him?” Peggy began looking around the boxes and chairs in the storage room. “He’s too short to reach the doorknob, so he has to be in here somewhere.”

As the door chimes jingled, Arlene stifled a chuckle. “Maybe that’s him now!”

Peggy moaned and brushed off her knees before following Arlene out into the store.

“Hey there, Cora. How are you?” Arlene smiled as her eyes darted around the room, hoping the bells on the door would bring out the pup.

“Hello ladies. I’m doing well. I just dropped by to pick up Violet Hoenigberg’s yarn order. She said it was ready.”

“It is. I left her a voice mail, but I knew she’d been out-of-town visiting her daughter, so I put it in the back. Let me get it.” Arlene held up a finger. "I'll be right back."

"Peggy, Violet is back in town now, and when she called to let me know she'd arrived home safely, I told her about the dress you found. It's been on my mind since I read that obituary you showed me, so I asked her what she remembered about Olive. We were both teaching when that happened, and I know Violet helped her with one of her plays."

"It's been on my mind as well." Peggy looked around the room quickly and turned back to Cora. "I remember her class performed in one of the Christmas plays."

"Yes, Violet has a lovely voice of her own, too." Cora Mae frowned when Peggy continued to wander around the aisles. "She told me that the riff between Olive and Eleanor was more than just jealousy over Olive being selected as the lead of the drama club. She said Eleanor actually filed a complaint against the school about it."

"Really? I guess she didn't win that."

"They didn't change their mind about their

selection, so then she got an attorney and filed it with the State Board of Education."

"Wow! What did they do?"

"Apparently, it takes years for that kind of thing to be resolved and it was still pending when Olive died. Violet didn't think she ever got a final ruling, but she said Eleanor was not likely to win, anyway."

"Eleanor would have had seniority at the school."

"Yes, but that's not the deciding factor in our district. They promote on merit and Eleanor had a lot of complaints from parents and other teachers on her record. She can be rather difficult to get along with, and you know Olive had a delightful disposition. The kids loved her."

"She was always cheery." Peggy's eyes darted inside the revolving metal stand of buttons and zippers. "I'm not surprised the kids responded well to her."

"Am I interrupting something?" Cora Mae began to look around the room, too, but found nothing out of the ordinary.

"Found it!" Arlene came through the curtains that covered the storage room door with a large white bag.

"No." Peggy shook her head. "We were just in the back putting together a pet crate for the puppy when you came in."

"Oh!" Cora squealed. "He's here! Can I see him? I've heard all about him from Amanda."

"Well," Arlene handed the bag to Cora Mae. "You can if you can find him. He seems to be hiding from us at the moment."

"The little rascal. You can't trust him for a minute." Peggy forced a smile, but worry was setting in across her face.

"Rascal is a cute name. I remember when Bing and I got married, he had an aunt and uncle that had a schnauzer named Rascal." Cora Mae hummed with a grin. Memories of those early years always warmed her heart.

"Violet ordered that by phone, and she's already paid for that order." Arlene walked behind the counter and sat on the high stool behind the cash register. "Is she doing okay? I haven't seen her since early December."

"Yes, she's just tired from the flight and has a lot to do. I told her I'd pick this up for her and bring it to church with me on Sunday."

"I talked to Danny Wittig briefly last night, and I told him about the dress I found. He said he'd let me look through the storage room where all the drama props and costumes are stored. I'm planning to run out to the high school in a few minutes."

"Wonderful idea!" Cora Mae reached for the doorknob. "I should be getting back. I hope you find the pup soon. I'd love to meet him!"

"Bye, Cora." Arlene waved as Cora pulled the door shut and then looked at Peggy. "What are we going to do? Where could he be?"

Peggy put her hands on her hips and huffed. "Can't you call him or something?"

"Call him what? He doesn't have a name."

"Whistle." Peggy nodded, waiting for Arlene to respond.

"I can't whistle."

"Me either." Peggy scowled and then they both laughed. "I'm going to the high school. If you haven't found him by lunchtime, maybe the smell of food will draw him out."

"Good idea!"

# Chapter 9

Sitting patiently in her car, Peggy looked around the high school grounds. She had texted Danny that she was outside, per his instructions, and was waiting to see him come out the door. He had warned her that he was hard to find during the day and he was afraid she might be trampled if she walked in when the kids were changing classes. Within minutes she saw him pop outside and wave his arms at her.

Meeting on the sidewalk out front, Peggy looked anxiously at the school. "Is it safe in there?"

Danny laughed with a twinkle in his eye.

"You've come at the most opportune time! They've just settled into third period, so we have about thirty minutes of peace. Come on in."

"It's been years since I've been here and then it was in the evenings. I used to attend the school plays and help out when I could, but that's been many years ago."

"I think you'll find that nothing has changed." Danny held the door open for Peggy to walk through, and the smell engulfed her with memories.

"Is the drama storage still at the end of the hall?"

"It sure is." Danny pointed as he pulled keys from his pocket.

"Does Eleanor know I'm here? I don't want to be in the way." Peggy looked both ways down the hall before following Danny into the room.

"I didn't tell her, but you won't see her. She's teaching a class this hour."

Peggy took a deep breath and nodded.

"This stuff doesn't belong to her. It

belongs to the school, so it's no concern of hers. If you find something that you made here or that you think could be useful to the community center, you are welcome to take it. We don't even use ninety percent of all this. It's just built up over the years. I've been here three years and Eleanor has not yet put on a school play."

Peggy leaned back. "Really? Why not?"

"Oh, I mean they do skits for pep rallies and work on presentations in drama class, but a play that the public can come to, no. She keeps saying they aren't ready."

"She does understand that they graduate, doesn't she?" Peggy chuckled. "I mean, I understand working on improving them, but they only get one chance, one year to do it."

Danny nodded sternly. He had given her an ultimatum this year to have a Christmas play, and she told him that if she did, she would have to withdraw from the community center because she didn't have the time to do both. Danny hadn't wanted to hurt the planned community presentations, but next year, he was not giving in.

“If she doesn’t like doing plays, I wonder why she volunteers at the center.” Peggy’s eyebrows knitted together in confusion. Eleanor wasn’t afraid to take charge of those, yet wouldn’t use her students, who had signed up to perform. The actors in the community were no more trained than the students, perhaps less.

“Here are the costumes.” Danny pushed some boxes aside to pull a rolling rack into the center of the room with an assortment of costumes on hangers. “Each costume has a number pinned to it and there is a corresponding box on the shelf there with the props that go with it.”

Peggy’s head turned to see rows of white boxes, each with a large number written in black marker. “You are so organized!”

“Oh, no. It wasn’t me. I’m told the previous drama teacher arranged all of this.”

“That was Olive. Olive Vogel was the director before Eleanor. Have you heard of her?"

Danny closed his eyes briefly and nodded. "The ladies in the office were very fond of her. I've heard many good things."

"She was well liked by the students, too. She's been on my mind since Eleanor gave me that dress."

"Oh, Eleanor gave it to you? I thought someone performing in the play brought it in."

"Well, yes. They brought it to Eleanor and then she contacted me. The actress needs it altered."

"Ah," Peter held his finger up. "Eleanor didn't recognize it?"

"No, but I didn't either at first. It's nothing special. Just a fancy dress that was originally made for 'My Fair Lady', I think. It was pretty at the time. It's showing its age now, just as I am."

Danny smiled. "Well, I hope you can find a use for something here. Everything is just gathering dust."

"Danny, has anyone mentioned to you that

Eleanor was quite angry when Olive was given her position as the drama teacher?"

"Oh, yes. I've heard the stories." Danny's eyes widened. The office ladies had told a few tales.

"I mention it only to warn you that Eleanor filed complaints back then. She is not afraid to fight against decisions she doesn't agree with. I'm assuming that litigation is moot now."

"I guess so. The board has never brought it up to me, so it was probably dismissed when Olive passed away."

"Now that you mention it, I don't remember Eleanor being involved at all in the plays that Olive put on. You would think someone who loved teaching drama would want to participate in some manner."

"Perhaps it was the clash of their personalities that prevented it."

"Perhaps, but if Eleanor didn't like Olive, she was the only person I've ever known to feel that way."

Danny pulled the door open. "Take your

time, but if you hear a bell ring, give it fifteen minutes before you try to escape."

Peggy laughed as Danny looked fearfully out the door before walking into the hall as she began her search.

Pushing boxes around, Peggy peered into one and then another. There were swords, fanciful hats, and common household goods of all varieties. The few costumes hanging on the rolling rack were not familiar to Peggy and must have been acquired after Olive's death. Eleanor had never asked for Peggy's help with school plays, and now she knew why.

Pulling down a box with a feather poking out of the top, Peggy saw the plastic hook that Olive had used for Captain Hook in Peter Pan. That had been a fun production, and the blue dress Nina brought to her had been altered and used for Wendy. It was all coming back to her now.

Checking her watch, she thought she had time for a getaway before the bell rang, so she stepped out into the hallway and made certain the storage room door was locked.

"Hi, Peggy!"

Startled, Peggy looked up and saw Marsha Kent walking towards her. "Hi! You know, I was just saying to Arlene that I hadn't seen you in a long time."

"I know," Marsha shook her head. "I've just been too busy to do anything lately. The holiday season this year was exhausting, and I don't seem to have any time for myself anymore."

"Well, Arlene and I were talking about Olive Vogel this week. Someone found an old costume that I made for Olive way back and we've been reminiscing."

"Oh, my." Marsha placed her palm over her heart. "I miss her so much."

"I know you two were good friends, so you might be able to help me. After finding that dress, I've been on a hunt for the other costumes. The community center could sure use them. If I could find them, they could be altered for future productions. That's why I'm here. Danny let me look around, but they aren't here."

"No, she always kept them at home."

"Any idea where they might be now?"

"I guess Ralph has them." Marsha's tone did not hide her negative feelings for the man. "Unless he threw them out." Shaking her head, she lifted her chin. "One of the boys might know. They are both living back in town now."

"Yes, I've heard that, but I haven't talked with them yet."

"Ralph wasn't easy to get along with, so I don't know if the boys talk to him." Marsha huffed. "He only thought about himself, and I know Marty didn't get along with Ralph at all, even as a kid."

"I don't mean to sound nosy, but hunting for these dresses has stirred all this up for me. I can't stop thinking about Olive and the accident. I loved her as much as everyone else, and I just don't think the accident was investigated properly. There must be something more we could learn. Did she talk about her home life with you? About the boys and about her husband?"

"The boys especially. As Marty got older, she worried about who he hung around with and Doug was always trying to be like Marty, but the two boys are nothing alike. She worried about Doug struggling to make friends and sometimes the boys fought. Just normal mom stuff, but I always told her girls are worse!" Marsha smiled.

"How was her relationship with Ralph?"

Marsha looked down at the floor and thought about her answer for a few seconds, as if she struggled to find the correct label. "Distant."

"Did she talk about divorce?" Peggy whispered. "I did hear a lot of gossip about Ralph."

"No. They just didn't talk to each other. I think they just coexisted, and it frustrated her because she felt he neglected the boys. She had to do everything, and he lived like a single man."

"Did she think Ralph was having an affair?"

"Probably, but it wasn't his first and I don't really think she cared. If he had just been a decent dad, she would have ignored his running around."

Peggy frowned. "So, why do you think she was driving out of town that night?"

Marsha's eyes dropped down again, and she twisted her hands together. "I don't know for certain."

"No one does, but I'd like to hear what you think it could have been about. I know you are tortured with her loss, too."

Marsha pushed her hair behind her ear and toyed with the button on her sweater before glancing up at Peggy. "I'm not sure, but she could have been going out to Nancy Whitehead's house."

"But why would she do that if she didn't care if Ralph was there?" Peggy shrugged.

"Not for Ralph. I think she wanted to talk to Nancy."

"It was pretty late, though. If she just wanted to talk to Nancy, wouldn't she call her or visit earlier?"

Marsha exhaled loudly. "The day of the accident, I picked Olive up for work because Ralph needed the car."

Peggy nodded for encouragement.

"Olive, well everyone, had heard rumors that Nancy Whitehead was pregnant. That made Olive very angry. She believed it. I mean, there was no reason not to believe it. Olive knew Nancy and Ralph were seeing each other, but a baby was a whole different thing."

Peggy nodded. "I did hear that rumor back then, but I'd forgotten about that. Why did that change things so much for Olive?"

"Because he wasn't being a dad to the child he had!" Marsha threw her hands out in front of her, obviously in support of Olive's reaction. "She wanted to warn Nancy, tell her what to expect. In the beginning Ralph had promised to be a dad to Marty, and then Olive and Ralph had a child of their own. He didn't even take care of his own, let alone do anything other than fight with Marty constantly."

"That makes sense. Olive would worry about someone else making the mistake she had, and she was probably even worried about the unborn child. She always put everyone else first." Peggy wasn't sure where parental concern ended and jealousy began.

"She thought the boys would suffer even more from it, knowing Ralph went off and had another child outside their family."

"So, Olive was trying to reach Nancy?"

"She had called more than once already and left messages for her at work. Nancy wasn't calling her back."

"So, you think she was driving out there? It was really late."

"Maybe they did finally talk, and they fought?" Marsha tossed her hands up and shrugged. "I don't know what transpired, but I know she had been trying to reach her, and she had called her. There's nothing else out that far on Rosemary Road, unless...."

Peggy took a deep breath and waited.

"Unless Ralph was out there and called her to come. The boys were at home and there was no reason she would leave them home at that hour and drive out a country road unless she was headed to see Nancy or Ralph."

"It's puzzling to me, too. Maybe we'll never know."

"I wonder what Ralph's story was." Marsha glowered with disdain.

"I heard the reports say he was playing cards at someone's house."

"I think she heard that one a lot," Marsha smirked. "It was another excuse to explain where he went at night."

"Did you ever hear if the rumor was true? Was Nancy Whitehead pregnant?"

"If she was, she lost it, because they never had a child together."

Peggy closed her eyes and nodded. "So sad. If you think of anything that might help, call Chief Harris at the police department. I've been talking to him about it, and he'd want to know anything you can remember."

"I will." Marsha squeezed Peggy's hand. "And I'll come see you at the store real soon! Tell Arlene I said hello."

"I will!" Peggy waved as she hurried down the hallway. She had to hurry, so she didn't get trapped by the class bell.

---

"Good afternoon, boys." Cora Mae smiled as Conrad walked into her office with Officer Briscoe on a leash. "Out for a stroll?"

"Yeah, on this lovely day." Conrad huffed as he dropped into the padded armchair across from Cora's desk. The weather had been dismal, overcast and cold all week. "Briscoe should have been a postal dog. He wants to walk in rain, sleet or hail. I can't say I'm in the same frame of mind."

"I'm ready for some sunshine myself." Cora pulled open her bottom desk drawer and

Briscoe's ears twitched.

"Come see, Aunt Cora." Cora motioned to Briscoe, and he glanced at Conrad.

"It's okay." Conrad shook his head. "You've got to stop giving him treats, or he's going to move in here."

"I want him to enjoy his visits here." Cora patted Briscoe on the head before he returned to Conrad's side.

"He's already had one treat on his walk. We ran into Saucy on the way here and he always has a dog treat in his pocket."

"Aw, that's sweet. Does he carry it just in case he runs into you?"

"No, he said he carries it in case he gets chased." Conrad laughed. "He walks around town a lot, and I guess he doesn't want to come across a stray that can outrun him."

Cora Mae laughed, too.

"The reason I'm here," Conrad unzipped his jacket and pulled out a file folder. "I wanted to show you something."

Cora took the folder Conrad handed her

and opened it on her desk.

"After you left the P.D., I asked Georgia to get the county file on that car accident. Since our file was so sketchy, I was curious."

"Oh, my." Cora was speechless. There were many more photos of the car and the driver's seat was non-existent. The crash had been head-on and it was clear no one could have survived it.

"You can't really tell it by looking at those, but if you go past the next couple...." Conrad stood up and pulled out a photograph taken at the garage after the car was towed. "Notice anything?"

Cora studied the photograph. "The back wheel is missing."

"Exactly! Now go back to the scene shots you just had." Conrad waited for Cora to find the earlier photos. "See the back wheel there?"

"It tilted out at an angle." Cora looked up at Conrad with a furrowed brow. "Did it come off when they towed it?"

"I don't think so. I think it was off at the

scene and the car was just pushed against it. You know, at first, I thought maybe the tie-rod snapped, but the pictures of it at the garage show the rod is intact."

"I don't understand."

"I think the wheel came off or was very loose when the wreck happened. I don't think it was because of the ice on the road. The weather and the pictures don't support it."

"What an unfortunate accident." Cora shook her head and began to read the narrative of the report. "I don't see anything mentioned about the wheel in here."

"No." Conrad shook his head. "I saw one report, I think it was Cantrell's, he mentioned it as an observation, but no other info."

"Well, what does that mean?" Cora put the report down and looked at Conrad. "Did they miss it completely?"

"I can only guess that they weren't trying to discern a cause. They were just addressing the situation. There was no one assigned to investigate, no interviews with the neighbors, and no detailed inspection of the car. Case closed."

"Are you telling me that you think there might have been another car involved?"

"No." Conrad waved his hand. "I don't see any damage to the vehicle that's unexplained. If it had been my case, I would have talked to the neighbors in the area to see if anyone had heard anything. The time estimate is pretty broad because they don't know when it happened."

"I hope she didn't suffer." Cora Mae swallowed and passed the folder back to Conrad.

"It gives me a bad feeling. There are things here that weren't addressed, and that gets under my skin. They wrote it up like it was just an all gas and no brake accident. Those kinds of accidents happen to people impaired or reckless. Olive doesn't sound like the type to be either."

"I agree."

"I would have asked the family if the car had been worked on recently or if they'd had any car trouble. I would have looked for the lug nuts to see if they were at the scene. I would have had someone put the car on a lift and look under it. The file doesn't indicate anyone questioned anything at all." Conrad let his hands fall to slap against his thighs. "I pulled the file to put my mind at ease, and it's done just the opposite."

"There's nothing to prevent you from talking with her husband or her sons now. Ralph remarried, but he lives here in town. Both of her boys are back here now, too. Maybe Sergeant Cantrell remembers it. You could make some inquiries."

"I've thought about it. I'm sure my questions won't be welcomed by any of them at this late date."

"You know what they say," Cora Mae tilted her head toward Conrad. "What is right is not always popular."

"As I've grown older, I've learned that pleasing everyone is impossible." Conrad shrugged. "However, ticking everyone off is a piece of cake!"

Cora Mae smiled in agreement.

Standing up, Conrad shook Briscoe's leash for him to rise. "I'll think on it some more."

Sheri Richey

# Chapter 10

"That was quick!" Arlene's head popped up when Peggy walked into the store from the back door. "Did you find anything out there?"

"Not much. I saw a couple of costumes that I remember altering, but nothing that I made. I did see a lot of newer props and cheap store-bought costumes, that Olive would never have used. I don't know why the stuff is there at all."

"Maybe Eleanor had her own collection of items that she's added since you helped Olive with the holiday programs."

"No. That's the weird thing about it. Danny said Eleanor has never done a school play, not one since she took over the drama department. I was shocked."

"What does a drama director do if there are no plays?" Arlene raised her eyebrows.

"I guess she's teaching acting. I don't know." Peggy shrugged. "Danny didn't elaborate, but I got the impression he wasn't happy about it. At night, she's downtown directing a town play and won't do a single one for the school."

"I can't understand that."

"So, where's the dog? After all that work to get the cage together and then he disappears!" Peggy scowled at Arlene's helpless expression and tossed her hands up. "He must have gotten out somehow."

Arlene shook her head. "I have a hair appointment and I was going to take him to the shelter before I went to the beauty shop."

"You were?"

Peggy's shocked expression made Arlene feel even worse. "I just don't know what else to do. I thought I could find him a home and I've failed him. I've done everything short of putting him on the front page of the newspaper and no one will give him a chance. I've called every friend I can think of and shown him to everyone I've seen."

"What about Cece Fields at the library? Did you ask her?"

Arlene huffed. "I went down to the library with him, but Cece said she actually thinks he's ugly! Can you believe that? She might have been joking, but I was so hurt I just left without looking for Elsie. I think Elsie has cats, but I was going to ask for her help, too."

"Well, you did the best you could. Shelby will make sure he finds a home."

"I know, but I hate to think of him caged up down there with all that big dog chaos. I'm afraid he'll be frightened. He's so small. Hymie said he was probably only eight to ten weeks old. I can't believe I've lost him."

"You can go on over to the beauty shop and I'll keep my eyes open. I appreciate you stopping by to cover for me so I could run out to the school. I'll text you if he turns up."

Arlene grabbed her jacket and purse. "It's just a trim. I'll be back soon."

---

"Good morning, boys." Ella Quinn walked into the bay at Wade's Garage and batted her eyes playfully to the workers nearby. She knew them all by name from making frequent trips down there for inspections and repairs of the used cars on her lot. She even hired them away from Wade once in a while, just as she had Marty Nash.

A chorus of voices said, "Morning, Miss Ella."

"Don't get too excited now. I'm just here to check on my cars." Ella smiled and strolled past them, doing her best Mae West impression, which made the young men chuckle. "Where's the old man at?"

Fingers pointed toward the office, and Ella

winked as she walked away. The old man was Wade Henry, owner of Wade's Garage, and he was actually younger than Ella Quinn, but she would never acknowledge that.

"Morning, Wade. Marty called and said my car was ready, so I'm here to settle up." The first vehicle, with a side dent, had been repaired easily and was already back on the lot. The car Marty had been driving, however, had grill and headlight damage, so it had been more involved.

"Yep, she's ready to go." Wade handed her a bill and leaned back in his creaking desk chair, waiting for the haggling to begin. Ella never just accepted a bill the first time around.

"Now, look here, Wade Henry. We had a deal. I gave you little Marty back for a week and he fixed his mistakes. I understand he took up a bay and used your tools, but this is a lot more than a rental fee."

"Now, Ella, you know that boy can't fix all that alone. He's not that skilled at body work and we had to replace some parts that weren't easy to find for a late model car. I had to get

Freddy on it to do some calling around." Freddy's Automotive was a part shop on the south side of Spicetown. "Quentin Radford did most of the work, and he's my best man."

"I understand the cost of parts, but our deal was half labor, and this is more than that." Ella shifted her weight and put one hand on her hip. "Don't take me for a fool, Wade Henry. I'll take my business someplace else. I won't stand around and let somebody cheat me!"

Wade chuckled. He had intentionally marked it up, so he'd have room to bring the price down for her. Ella wasn't satisfied unless she thought she had won the deal. Reaching for the bill, he pretended to study it and then crossed through the price to offer the agreed-upon amount.

Ella grabbed it from Wade's hand when he held it out and pretended to consider it before handing it back. "That's more like it." Ella sat down in the chair across from Wade and pulled her billfold from her purse.

"So, how's little Marty working out for you

down there?" Wade didn't harbor any ill feelings for Ella taking Martin Nash out of his employ. Marty could do the work with supervision, but he wasn't a natural like his daddy had been.

"Hard to say," Ella huffed. "He's not done much but wreck a couple of cars so far."

"I admit, I was curious if he could be a good salesman for you. He's not that strong with talking at people, you know."

"He does seem a bit shy and nervous. I'm hoping I can break him in a little with time. Dwight tells me he's hotheaded, but I haven't seen that from him yet."

"Yep, he can blow off sometimes. You might want to be careful about pushing him too far. He don't take teasing too good. The guys here would joke around with him, and it would set him off. Then he sulks for days after." Wade shook his head. "It made things tense out there for a while, so the guys just started staying away from him. To tell you the truth, I wasn't sorry he decided to go try selling cars for a while."

"Sometimes it takes people a little while to find their right place in the world. I don't know what all he's tried so far." She had bounced around a long time looking for her niche and had been in her forties before everything clicked for her.

"He's moved around a bit, tried different things. He lived in Indiana when he got out of the military and worked for a moving company for a few years. That's a young man's job though, so he tried working on farm equipment in Kentucky, but those combines don't run like an Army truck." Wade chuckled. "It was like he was trying not to come home, but when his daddy's health declined, I think that's what got him back here. Billy Nash worked a long time for me and when he called and said his boy needed a job, I couldn't turn him down."

"I guess we'll have to see how it goes."

Wade handed Ella a receipt for her check. "Good luck!"

---

Since the store was empty, Peggy gathered up her packing slips from the new merchandise she had received in the last couple of days and stacked them by the computer in the back room. If she pinned the curtain back, she could keep an eye on the front door while she updated her inventory records. She still didn't feel like all of her pending orders had been filled.

Bracing herself for the balance she knew was on her business spreadsheet, she was reminded of the talk she still needed to have with Arlene. She wasn't looking forward to that.

When she clicked open her accounting software, her elbow brushed the stack of receipts and one floated to the floor as she groaned at the display. Spinning her chair sideways, she leaned over to grab it and glanced at the three-tiered shelf beside her work desk.

Curled up comfortably on a folded remnant of camel-colored fleece she had used to make a March lion for her store display was the plump brown puppy perfectly camouflaged and sound asleep. He was snoring comfortably, resting his head on a fuzzy piece of cream trim.

Peggy studied his little pink paws and white stomach, itching to touch him, but not wanting to wake him, she took a picture with her phone to text to Arlene with the caption, 'Sitting like a knickknack on the shelf'.

# Chapter 11

Seeing the curtain tacked back, Arlene knew Peggy must be in the back and she called out to Peggy when she walked through the door. "It's just me." Hanging up her jacket, she looked down at the puppy in the crate. "I see he woke up."

"He did. I can't keep an eye on him every minute, so I put him in there."

Arlene squatted down and poked her finger into the cage so the pup could chew on it. "He needs some toys."

"We need some lunch!" Peggy spun around in her chair. "Vicki called and said she'd come over for lunch today. Dorothy's club sandwich is today's special so I told her to go ahead and put in our order. I hope you don't mind."

"Not at all. That sounds wonderful! Can I do anything to help while we wait?"

"No, I was just putting these receipts in. I'm still missing several items, so I sent them an email. Your hair looks nice."

Arlene fluffed her hair with her hand. "I had Louise cut it a little shorter, hoping it would trigger the weather to warm up."

"While we're waiting, I wanted to talk to you about work hours for the spring." Peggy had stewed this over in her mind all evening. "I expect business will decrease, at least for the next few months. It always does this time of year."

"That's true." Arlene reached into the small refrigerator in the storage room to get out drinks for both of them. "I'm glad you brought that up because I've been thinking about that, too. Mavis and her egg apron have been on my mind. Cora Mae asked a few weeks ago if we had any new craft ideas for a Saturday project at the community center. We haven't done one since early December and they've always been popular, but we probably need a new idea."

Peggy nodded. They were well attended, but they were so much work. She wasn't sure it ended up being profitable in the end, and she would really struggle to do something like that alone.

"Spring wreaths would probably be okay. We had good attendance at the fall wreath event, and everyone might be looking for something cheery to make for the front door."

Peggy nodded again, waiting for an opening in the conversation to turn her way.

"But what about painting flowerpots? We've never done that, and everyone will be ready to start decorating their porch and gardening. We could also have a sewing table to make a garden apron. They have easy patterns for a pocketed apron like Mavis' except instead of eggs, you can put your trowel and pruners in them. It's like a tool belt for the yard! What do you think?"

"Well..."

"Either project seems too small alone, but if we combine them, we will open the door of opportunity to more people. They could even bring their kids to paint while the moms cut out patterns for the aprons. We could even incorporate some practical crochet, like cotton towel toppers, soap mitts, or hot pads. Just make different stations for small projects. It would be something for everyone!"

Peggy scowled. "Arlene, we'd have to take the whole store across the street for all that!"

"What if we made kits that they could pick from? We would already have everything together for them. That might even be good for the store. We could create some simple sewing kits or crochet projects now."

"That's a lot of work for us."

"Yes, but once the new stock is out, we'll have time during the day. I also thought about a kids' craft day after school gets out. People will always spend money on their kids. I love making ribbon flowers and we can paint Popsicle stick projects or use paper plates to trace on and paint pictures. There are a million things we could do for kids and they're all really simple."

Peggy laughed. "I'm exhausted just listening. Where do you get all this energy?" Peggy realized then that she paid Arlene for more than just her hours of work, but also for her innovative ideas and pure positive energy that she needed now more than ever.

"I'll help! We can do it! It'll be fun!" As if on cue, the pup yipped at Arlene's enthusiasm just as the front bell jingled.

"Lunch has arrived!" Vickie Garwin elbowed her way in the door with three lunch boxes stacked up and a drink in her hand. "Here you go, ladies. Where shall we sit?"

Arlene motioned Vicki to the back of the store.

"They are all the same, except the one with the extra pickle is Arlene's." Vickie chuckled. "Dorothy told me the pickle was very important."

"It is!" Arlene smiled. "Dorothy is so good to me."

"So, tell me what you both have going on. It's so nice to finally have someone working for me that I can trust. It's been years since I felt like I could leave for lunch."

"Have you hired someone new?" Peggy placed a stack of napkins on the coffee table.

"Hannah Arnett. She's been there about three months so far and she's been such a help to me. She's worked in a bakery before. Her uncle owns Kneady Delights over in Red River. Have you heard of it? It's a tiny shop near the railroad track, but it's been there forever. Her uncle does all the baking, but she learned so much just watching and helping him."

"That's wonderful! Are you teaching her to bake?" Arlene glanced toward the back room when she heard the puppy's tiny yip. "I bet he can smell the food."

"Oh, yes, the puppy! Peggy told me about him. Is he in the back?" Vicki jumped up and carried her lunch to the storage room doorway to peek at him. "He's a little dumpling, isn't he?"

"He's something," Peggy gritted her teeth. "Worked us into a panic this morning when we thought we lost him."

Arlene shared the story and photo with Vicki.

"What's the latest on the dress? Did you go to the school today?" Vicki took a sip of tea and turned to Arlene. "Peggy told me about the old dress last night when I ran into her outside of the community center."

"I did, but I didn't find anything out there. I guess they're all gone."

"You know, you should ask your new neighbor." Vicki pointed next door. "Olive's son might know. At least he might know where she kept them."

"I haven't met him yet." Peggy winced. "I know. I need to go over there."

"He's been in the bakery. He's dating my new assistant, Hannah."

"Is she blonde?" Arlene squinted her eyes. "I saw a young blond leaving the barbershop one afternoon as I walked out."

"That's her. I don't think they've dated long, but that may be the reason she chose to work in Spicetown. I couldn't understand at first why she just didn't work for her uncle, but she seems very interested in Doug. I don't know if the feeling is mutual."

"Well, you better make sure they don't break up!" Peggy chuckled. "You could lose your assistant."

"That's my concern. She's still living over that way. I'll feel better once she moves here."

"So, what do you think of Doug?" Peggy pointed at Arlene with a potato chip in her hand. "Arlene went over and met him."

"Yes, but he barely spoke to me. I had to do all the talking. Either he didn't want company or he's painfully shy."

"Socially awkward." Vickie raised her eyebrows. "I don't think he's much of a communicator. At least that was my take. I've tried to chat him up a couple of times without success. It's odd, because Hannah is just as chatty as a macaw. I guess she keeps the conversation flowing."

Arlene nodded in agreement. "I didn't stay there long. It was difficult to be alone with him."

"It's going to be hard to run a business and not talk to customers." Peggy didn't find it to be the easiest thing to do either sometimes, especially when she really wasn't in the mood.

"He needs another barber in there with him. That would help." Arlene crunched on her pickle. "He probably had a challenging time as a kid. Losing your mother so young must be devastating."

"Growing up with Ralph is no walk in the park, either." Vicki closed up her lunch box. "Marty left, but Doug was too young. He was trapped there and then Ralph married Nancy Whithead right away, so he had a new stepmother to adjust to."

Peggy groaned. Nancy was a contrary

customer that couldn't be pleased. "I don't see Nancy much anymore. She used to come in here and complain about my selection and prices. She always told me how much better online shopping was. I think she must just buy online now."

"She was here once before Christmas to get some green ribbon for something, but I didn't even realize she was married to Ralph Vogel. She still uses the name Whitehead." Arlene closed her lunch box and set it aside. "I didn't know she was married."

"Maybe they didn't marry," Vicki shrugged. "Or she didn't take his name because they married so quickly, but I know she moved into a new house right away. Almost as if it was all planned."

Peggy's eyes widened. "Olive's death?"

"Maybe not death, but I got the impression Ralph had the relationship going before Olive's accident. It happened too fast for any other explanation." Vicki shook her head. "Billy cheated on her, too."

"Dorothy told me that her first husband, Billy Nash, was not a great pick, either."

"That's an understatement. Thankfully, she got away from him quickly. He was a heavy drinker, and it didn't improve his personality."

"Do you know the other son, Marty?" Arlene gathered up the lunch debris, saving a sliver of ham for the pup.

"Not well, but he's been in the bakery. He's married now and working out at Ella's car lot, Cajun Motors. I only know that because she called in the order he picked up one morning, and I asked him if he worked there. He's only been back in town a couple of years. Both boys have been gone for at least ten years, but I don't know where they were."

Peggy hummed. "I wonder if they were together or if they're close."

"Tragedy can draw people together." Arlene walked over to the puppy's cage to give him a piece of ham and bring him over to meet Vicki. "Meet our latest tragedy." Arlene held the pup up and he wiggled all over when she held him out.

Peggy chuckled. “He is a hard-luck case. Arlene has called everyone, and she can’t find him a home.”

“Why can’t he stay here?” Vicki held her hands up. “It’s the perfect place! I wish I could bring my dog to work with me.” Seeing Peggy’s eyes shoot daggers at her, Vicki rose up onto her feet. “Well, I need to get back. Thanks for lunch, girls. See you soon.”

# Chapter 12

"Good morning, this is Conrad Harris over at the Spicetown P.D. Is Sergeant Cantrell working today, by any chance?"

"Morning, Chief. Yeah, he's here today. Let me put you on hold, and I'll see if I can find him for you."

"Thank you." Conrad picked up his pencil and read through the questions he hoped to ask. He'd given this a lot of thought and although this wasn't official Spicetown business, he wouldn't be able to ignore the questions in his mind about what really happened that night in February, 2002. If Cantrell didn't remember the scene, he would be at the end of his journey and could let it go, but he had to ask.

"Hey there, Chief! How are you? Everything okay in Spicetown?"

"Doing well. Thank you. Are you busy? I don't want to keep you from anything important."

"Nah, just pushed everyone out the door for shift change. I've got a few minutes. How can I help you?"

"Well, this is a big ask, but I was wondering if you remembered a one-car accident that happened just outside Spicetown on Rosemary Road back in February of 2002. I know that sounds crazy, but I just thought—."

Sergeant Cantrell stopped Conrad with a somber statement. "Olive Vogel."

"Yes! You do remember. I saw your name in the reports, but that was a long time ago."

"She was a schoolteacher over there. A young woman..."

"Yes. She was 36, had two sons. I wasn't around back then, but from what I hear, she was a pretty popular teacher and well liked by everyone."

"I was just a rookie back then; I hadn't even been on the road two years yet. She was my first fatality."

Conrad remembered his first as well.

"I was running around calling people, trying to find someone to tell me what I should be doing." Cantrell gave a feeble chuckle.

"And now you're the one the rookies are calling for help."

"Yes, the tables do turn with time. I sure hope I can do a better job for them than what I got that night."

"Did they leave you hanging?"

"They sent me more rookies! The hour was late, and you don't always get the best at that hour. None of us were experienced in handling that kind of scene. I kept feeling like I should be doing something more, but I didn't know what that was. I was a little rattled by it. It still haunts me, and that's why I remember her name."

"We all have our ghosts. When I read the reports, I couldn't help but think about all the things I would have done if I'd been there, and I wondered why they weren't done. I guess you've answered that question for me, though. I do understand. That happens to all of us sometimes."

"What brought the case to your attention?"

"Well, the boys have moved back to town now and the local gossip got stirred up a bit. I was just curious, so I looked up the report. Did you ever talk to the husband?"

"Not me. I wasn't assigned any follow-up, but I remember the station was trying to reach him and couldn't get a hold of him."

"I wonder if anybody followed up on it. I just can't help wondering where she was going or what caused the accident."

"I thought she just took the turn too fast. It's a tight corner right there."

"Yeah, but she was a local, and she knew that. It's not like she was rushing to get to an injured child or anything. Her kids were at home." Conrad tapped his pencil on his notepad. "I hope somebody at least did a tox screen. I've not heard she had any substance abuse issues, but that would help explain it."

"I can look in our files, if you like. If toxicology came back, they would have it in there."

"Would you? I'd appreciate it."

"Absolutely. You've got my curiosity up now."

Conrad chuckled. "Just one more thing, do you remember anything about the wheels on the car? I was looking at the pictures in our file from the scene."

"Yeah, the back wheel was off. I remember they had to get a flatbed to tow it. Didn't I put that in my report?" Sergeant Cantrell exhaled. "I bet I didn't. They were shuffling rookies all around the schedule and I didn't get a chance to write it up for a couple of days. I sure didn't take good notes at the scene, either. I was too shaken."

"It didn't look like the rod snapped. Do you remember any lug nuts on the tire or the ground?"

Sergeant Cantrell was silent for several seconds and then hummed with indecision.

"I know I'm asking a lot. I'm just trying to put my demons to sleep about it. I don't mean to wake yours up."

"Honestly, I don't think I even looked that closely at it. I don't remember anything about the wheel other than it was off. I learned a lot of lessons from that call."

"It's the only real way to learn this job."

"That's the truth!"

"Well, I won't keep you any longer. I appreciate your help." Conrad sat back, wondering what he could do if nothing more was recorded about that night than what he'd seen.

"I'll give you a call if I find out anything more."

"Thank you, Sergeant."

---

"Can I borrow the pup for a few minutes?" Peggy looked at Arlene. "I thought maybe I'd go next door and meet the neighbor. I can use the pup as a reason."

"Sure!"

"I can always ask him if he is interested in him. He's new to town, maybe he's looking for a pet."

"I don't know about that." Arlene frowned. "We don't really know him."

"What do you mean?"

"Well, I want him to go to a good home. I don't know if he has one."

Peggy rolled her eyes.

"He might be a little crazy. I can't just give the little doughboy to anybody."

"Oh, for goodness sakes! If he's interested, I'll tell him I need to check his references first. Would that help?"

Arlene hummed as she pretended to consider the option. "Throw in a home inspection, and I'll think about it."

"Deal! Come on chunky. Let's go meet the

new guy." Peggy lifted the pup from the crate, and he tried to lick her face. "Yuck."

"He's giving kisses!"

Peggy rolled her eyes again and chuckled. "I'll be back in a few minutes." Slipping out the front door, Peggy looked in the storefront window of the barbershop before trying the door. She could see the young man with the large ears cutting into boxes in the middle of the room. Two barber chairs were already in place in front of a rough counter frame that still lacked the countertop. It was shaping up slowly. Peggy tapped her knuckles on the glass door.

"Not open." Doug did not look up. He just yelled over his shoulder.

Peggy tapped again until he turned around. Pointing next door, she yelled, "I'm your neighbor."

Doug Vogel came to the door looking mildly annoyed, but he did not open the door. "Can I help you?"

"I'm Peggy. I own the shop next door."

Doug frowned, and Peggy started to think he wasn't going to respond. "I just wanted to introduce myself and say hello."

"Nice to meet you."

"May I come in?" Socially awkward was an understatement.

Doug sighed and unlocked the door but didn't move aside. "It's nice to meet you. There's nothing to see here, though. I'm just unpacking a few things."

"Oh, I'm not here to look around. I've seen the space. In fact, I considered buying it at one point. I just wanted to say hello and please feel free to come over if you need anything."

"Oh, okay."

"I believe you met Arlene a few days ago. She works for me."

"Yeah."

Peggy shuffled her feet and then remembered the puppy. "I don't suppose you are looking for a new pet, are you? We found this little guy in the alley behind the store, and he needs a good home."

Doug glanced down at the dog and quickly back up. “No. I’m not an animal person.”

“I don’t know if Arlene mentioned it, but we both knew your mother. In fact, most of the long-time residents in town probably did. She was a wonderful person. Her passing was so tragic.”

“Yeah.” Doug stood there expressionless.

“It must be nice to be back in your old hometown! I hear your brother is also back home. It must be great for your father to have everyone living close again.”

“We don’t have the same father.”

“Oh, yes, well, but you both have family connections here and we are all happy you’ve moved back. When do you expect to open?”

“I don’t know. It depends.” Doug shrugged.

“Well, the Spicetown Star is just a block over, north of Fennel Street, and when you’re ready to announce your opening, you can just write up an ad and Sally will make sure it’s in the paper. Just ask for Sally McGivens. She handles all the advertising there, and she's a very sweet lady. She knew your mother, too! I'm sure she'd be delighted to help you."

"Okay, thanks."

"I see you have two chairs. Will there be a second barber working here?"

Doug looked over his shoulder as if he had forgotten about the chairs. "I don't know yet."

"Have you thought of a name for your shop? You know, the town has a little bit of a theme and most of the merchants use a spice in their name somewhere."

"No, I haven't decided yet."

Peggy was plum out of ideas for conversation topics. "Well, as I said, I hope you'll come visit and let us know if you need anything."

Doug nodded and mumbled a quiet "Thanks" as he closed the door in her face.

# Chapter 13

"Socially awkward is an understatement." Peggy paced around the storeroom while Arlene got the crate ready for the puppy. "He wouldn't even let me in the door!"

"I didn't get much out of him either, but the door was unlocked the day I went over, so I just walked in."

Peggy pointed at the newspaper in the bottom of the dog crate and laughed. "You've got old Poison Poindexter in the right place!"

Arlene looked down and saw Ed Poindexter's picture with his editorial opinion column smiling up at her and snickered. "A perfect pee spot!" Arlene stood to reach for the puppy but stopped and cooed. "Aw, look at him. He's sound asleep."

Peggy tucked her chin and frowned, trying to look down at him. "Well, I guess I can hold him for a couple of minutes. Where is he spending the night?"

"Shelby said she would take him home with her for the night. She has a bunch of other dogs at home, but she said he would be okay."

"Doug said he isn't an animal person." Peggy raised her eyebrows. "I wasn't shocked to hear that. He's not a people person either."

Arlene nodded. "Well, Doug didn't even tell me his name or introduce himself at all to me after I told him who I was. It was a struggle to talk to him, so I don't think he'll be much of a source of information for you—about anything!"

"That was uncomfortable. I won't be going over there again. It was clear that he was not interested in neighborly camaraderie."

"Louise Morgan says the place will never open." Arlene chuckled. "You know Louise. She has the inside on everything and extra opinions to share."

"She knows Doug?" Peggy sat down on the couch and put a pillow under her elbow. The four-pound puppy suddenly seemed to weigh a ton.

"No, I think she's repeating things she's heard. She does know his brother, Marty, though. I think he may have gone to school with her son, and he worked on her car when he was at Wade's Garage."

"Yeah, Marty. I'm thinking he has to be easier to talk to. I wonder if he knows anything about his mother's belongings. He was older when she passed and maybe he knows what happened to her costumes."

"Louise said he works at Ella Quinn's place now, Cajun Motors. You could call him."

Peggy gritted her teeth. "And say what? It's kind of uncomfortable to talk about, you know. Hey, I used to know your mom. Do you know what they did with all her stuff when she died?"

"Yeah, I see what you mean. That speech

will take some work." Arlene laughed.

"I might be in the market for a new car!" Peggy hummed. "Maybe I should go take a test drive?"

"That's one way to ensure a captive audience." Arlene chuckled with a wary look. "Just remember what Dorothy told you, and don't make him mad!"

---

Cora Mae parked her car on Ginger Street to pick up her dry cleaning at the Peppercorn Dry Cleaners. She always took her winter wool coats in for cleaning at the end of the season, and even though the cool weather was lingering this year, she was hoping her actions would force the spring in.

"Sandy!" Cora tossed her hands up in surprise. "I didn't know you were working here now." Sandy Nash lived across the street from Cora Mae on Bay Leaf Boulevard with her husband, Marty.

"Hi, Mayor Bingham! Yes, I've been here about six months now, but I was in the back when I started. It was a great place to be in the winter. It's always toasty warm in here."

"That's true, but I don't know how great you'll feel about that this summer!" Cora Mae recalled when Sandy and her husband moved in across the street from her. She had shared her concerns about moving back to the cold winters when Cora had gone over to welcome them to the neighborhood. Sandy was raised in the area but had been living in Alabama for over a decade and had not missed the ice and snow.

Sandy laughed as Cora handed her the ticket for her coats. "Let me find your items."

"It's two coats," Cora called out to her as she moved the clothing racks around. "I'm trying to put winter behind me."

Sandy carried the coats covered in plastic to the front and hung them at the end of the counter. "I sure hope it works! I'm ready to plant flowers and do things outside. Marty bought a new grill at the end of the summer last year and I'd like to start using it."

"How is Marty? I haven't seen him for a while. I hear he has a new job."

"Yes! He's working at Cajun Motors now. He's only been there a short time, but I hope he likes it. He's never been a salesman before."

"Some people have a real knack for it. I know Ella Quinn will have a lot to teach him."

"Yeah, he says she's a smooth talker." Sandy smiled. "He doesn't think he can do it like she does, though."

"Everyone has to have their own style." Cora Mae winked. "How is Marty's dad doing? I know he's had some health challenges lately and hasn't been getting out at all."

"I haven't seen him." Sandy winced. "Marty checks on him sometimes, but they don't get along really well. His wife, Jeanie, seems very sweet."

"It's a shame you never got to meet Marty's mom. She was a wonderful lady." Cora Mae shook her head. "Her loss had a huge impact on a lot of people."

"Oh, I've heard a lot about her. When Marty talks about his childhood, it's always her that was at the center of things. He still has a hard time around the anniversary of her accident. It haunts him." Sandy put her hand over her heart. "I think it was because of how it happened. It was so traumatic for him."

"It was for all of us." Cora nodded. "Did he ever tell you why she was out on the road that night?"

"Looking for Ralph." Sandy rolled her eyes. "I'm sure Billy Nash was difficult to be married to, but Ralph was worse. Marty won't even speak to the man when we run into him. Technically, Ralph is still his stepfather, but he won't claim him. That's one of the reasons he hesitated to move back. He didn't want to run into Ralph, but he felt like he needed to be here for Billy. Billy told him he had a job at Wade's Garage if he would come back, and Marty felt like it was a sign his dad wanted him closer."

"Kind of offering an olive branch?" Cora Mae handed Sandy her credit card to pay for her cleaning.

"Yeah, I think he wanted to mend their relationship. They haven't been close over the years."

"Family is important." Cora Mae nodded. "And tomorrows are always uncertain."

"That's true." Sandy handed Cora her receipt and her card.

"Moving home also gives him a chance to catch up with his brother. I hear he's moved back and is opening a barbershop on Fennel Street soon. I haven't seen him yet, but I know others have told me he's hard at work on it."

"Doug?" Sandy scrunched up her shoulders and wrinkled her nose. "No, the brothers don't talk at all. I've never even met Doug. I keep wondering what will happen if we run into him."

"That's so strange! They were teenagers when their mom passed. If anything, you would have thought that would have made them closer to each other."

Sandy lowered her voice, although there

was no one else around. "You know, I actually think it was because they lost their mother. He talks as though they did get along as boys, but things changed once their mom was gone. Of course, it could have been because of Ralph, too. Marty and Ralph never got along."

"Yes, it would have been an awkward time for Marty." Cora hummed. "So close to adulthood but trapped in a home with a stepfather he didn't connect with."

"Yes, and Doug is close to Ralph. I mean, that's his dad!"

"I can see that their different feelings for Ralph could have pulled them apart, but it's sad."

"How did we get down this dark path?" Sandy feigned a chuckle and waved her hand. "Let's keep thinking positive spring thoughts!"

"Yes! Let's!" Cora smiled and waved as she turned toward the door.

# Chapter 14

Conrad Harris pulled open the door to the Old Thyme Italian Restaurant and held it for Cora Mae to enter. He had called and invited her for pizza before going to the play rehearsal.

Sliding into their usual booth, a waitress took their drink order and said their pizza would be right out. Conrad had called ahead to save time.

"I was surprised at your interest in pizza tonight." Cora Mae raised an eyebrow and smiled. "Are you working on a new case I don't know about?" Conrad rarely wanted pizza, but if he was thinking through something that perplexed him, it was his go-to meal.

Conrad chuckled. “I knew you would be suspicious.”

“Well?” Cora was not going to accept an evasive answer.

“It’s not a new case. It’s this Vogel thing.”

“Ah!” Cora Mae smiled with a twinkle in her eye. She had been right all along. “I’m glad you brought that up.”

“You are?”

Cora leaned back so the waitress could slide the pizza in front of them and hand them each a plate. “Let me know if I you need anything.”

“Thank you.” As the waitress backed away, they put a slice on their plates to cool.

“I don’t see Jo tonight.” Conrad looked around the restaurant for JoAnn Biglioni, the owner’s daughter. She usually greeted them at the door.

“She’s in Massachusetts.”

“Massachusetts!” Conrad scowled. He had just seen her a few days ago.

“Yes, her daughter is having a baby.”

"Oh." Conrad frowned. "Boy or girl?"

"Girl, I believe." Cora Mae opened her napkin and draped it over her lap.

"How's the weather up there?"

Cora Mae bristled. "Where? Massachusetts?"

"Yeah." Conrad shrugged. "You always know everything. I just figured you'd know that, too."

Cora Mae swung her arm out over the pizza and imitated a back-handed smack as they both laughed. "I'd give you a good whack for that if I could reach you."

"I know you would. That's why I said it when you couldn't." By the time they stopped laughing, the slices had cooled, and Conrad began eating.

"Okay, let me tell you about my trip to the dry cleaners today!"

"Sounds riveting." Conrad wiggled his eyebrows as Cora Mae laughed at herself.

"No, seriously now." Cora Mae inhaled deeply to put the silliness aside and told Conrad about her encounter with Sandy Nash in the Peppercorn Dry Cleaners earlier.

“I’m sure Ralph probably favors his own son over Olive’s, especially if he and Olive were having marital problems.”

“What makes you think they had marital problems?” Cora Mae took a bite of her pizza to catch up with Conrad. He had been eating the whole time she told her story.

“Sergeant Cantrell.”

“You talked to him today?”

“Twice. I called him this morning about the file. I asked him a few things, because he does remember working the scene. He was just a rookie back then, and I think he feels like the scene didn’t get handled thoroughly. Some of the questions I asked, he couldn’t answer, so he said he would try to pull their file on it.”

Cora Mae motioned for him to continue while she chewed.

“First, I asked him about the back wheel. He said it was completely off the car when they got ready to tow it. He remembers that because they had to get a flatbed tow instead of pulling it in."

"Did he send you the county's file on it?" Cora dabbed her mouth with her napkin.

"Yes, later he called back and told me there was a toxicology report in their file and it showed no drugs or alcohol in her system."

"You thought she was impaired?"

"We talked about a possible cause for the accident. She's a local. She's not reckless by nature. She shouldn't have missed that curve like that. Something else had to have been in play."

Cora nodded her agreement. Even the time of night had always left a question in her mind. "Did you ask him about Ralph? What story did he tell?"

"Cantrell didn't interview him, but the write-up was in the file. Ralph's story was he was at a buddy's house playing cards and stayed too late. He thought she might have been mad about it and was coming to get him."

"Without calling?" Cora scoffed.

"Everybody didn't have a cell phone back then."

"No, but they had a house phone. I don't think she knew where he was and was looking for him. Does this buddy live out on Rosemary Road?"

"Well, that's just it." Conrad pointed at Cora with his fork. "They didn't ask the name of this friend and they didn't verify his story."

"You need to talk to Ralph! Ask him where he was when she died. Find this so-called buddy and see if they corroborate this story."

"That's a little touchy." Conrad pushed his plate to the side. "There's no crime here, and investigating an accident that happened over twenty years ago isn't normal police procedure."

They sat in silence for several minutes and Cora Mae looked around the restaurant. "Ask the boys."

"What?"

"Ask the boys where Ralph was the night of the accident. Tell them you are tying up loose ends on old files from before your time, and you found the report incomplete. They were old enough to know what was happening that night."

Conrad shook his head and sighed. It still sounded like a thin excuse.

"I can't do it!" Cora Mae pointed at herself. "They'll just think I'm being nosy!"

Conrad chuckled. "I'll give it some thought. What do you know about Ralph?"

"He isn't well liked. That's the universal response from everyone I've talked to. He remarried right after Olive died and there was much speculation that Nancy had been rehearsing for the role."

Conrad frowned. "He was having an affair?"

"That was the gossip." Cora Mae pushed her plate to the side and asked the waitress for a refill of her tea.

"Maybe Olive was going to drive by Nancy's house. Did she live out that way?"

"Hmm, I don't know, but I might be able to tell from the water department records. I'll take a look tomorrow." Cora Mae pointed at Conrad and then picked up her phone to add the item to her list of things to do.

"It sounds like maybe Marty blamed Ralph for the accident and then Doug stuck up for his dad. That would explain the rift between the boys."

"That may have been. Everyone handles grief differently and sometimes people place blame on others for not grieving the way they do. I do wonder if Marty was troubled by Ralph before the accident or not. Although Ralph wasn't his father, he had lived with Ralph since he was a toddler. I don't think Billy Nash was a very active parent, so I would have expected Marty to view Ralph as his second dad, more than a stepparent."

"That long ago? I didn't realize she married Vogel when Marty was that young. It could have just been a personality clash. I hear Marty can be a little hot-headed like his dad and he could have butted heads with Ralph. The two boys are very different, I hear, and Ralph may have constantly compared the two, with Doug being the favored child."

"Yes, they were very different. Marty was outgoing and curious. Doug was very studious and introverted. Neither one has Olive's creative light-hearted nature." Cora took a sip of her tea and looked at her watch.

"Cantrell agreed with me that writing the accident off as possibly weather-related doesn't sit well. He didn't recall any patchy ice at all that night. I think he's a little upset with himself for not looking for the lug nuts for the tire. He saw the wheel was off, but his mind just didn't go there. He was too new at the job."

"I don't suppose it matters now. If they were missing completely or on the ground at the scene, the wheel coming off probably played a role in the accident since there was no evidence they broke. Isn't that true?"

Conrad nodded. "Both suggest negligence on someone's part."

"Or tampering." Cora tilted her head.

Conrad rapped his knuckles on the table.

"We better get over to the community center if you want a good seat to spy on Saucy."

"Spy on Saucy? Now, whatever gave you that idea?" Cora Mae chuckled as she scooted out of the booth and struggled into her jacket. Quietly she admitted, "Oh, you do know me so well."

"Who are you looking for?" Conrad looked over his shoulder at the random people milling about behind the auditorium seating. Cora kept looking over her shoulder, but Saucy was seated in the front row.

"Peggy. I thought she might drop by tonight with the dress she altered. I wanted to see how things are going with her hunt for the costumes."

"Has she asked Eleanor about it?" Conrad pointed toward the stage. "She may know if there are old costumes at the school."

"No, I don't think she has. She mentioned

it, but I suggested she not do that. At least not right away. Olive is a touchy topic with Eleanor. They were not friends."

Conrad nodded. "Saucy doesn't appear to be doing anything in this play. I'm not sure why he comes to rehearsals. He just sits there and watches them."

"I know I can't understand it! He must have a very small part. I don't know anything about this play, so I don't know what part he could have."

"What's it called again?" Conrad frowned. She had told him more than once, but he couldn't remember.

"Murder in the Heir. H-E-I-R."

"Maybe he's the guy that gets murdered?"

"Perhaps! That would be a great part for him. No lines to learn!"

"But you don't really need to rehearse for that." Conrad chuckled.

"Maybe he has a brief scene where he dies on stage and that's all."

"That could be." Conrad nodded. "Here

comes Eleanor."

"Good evening, Cora. Chief."

"Hi, Eleanor." Cora reached out her hand to stop her. "Can you tell me what role Saucy has this time? He's not been performing tonight."

"No, the part we're working on tonight isn't his scene. He doesn't have too many lines this time." Eleanor smiled, aware of Saucy's opening night anxiety from previous plays.

"Is he the guy that gets murdered?" Cora turned in her seat.

"No. That's Reuben Hobbs, Francine's husband. You know Reuben, don't you?" Eleanor looked around the room. "I don't see him at the moment, but he was here."

"Yes, I know them. So, what part does Saucy play?"

Eleanor smiled and turned to walk down the aisle. "You'll have to come to the play and find out!"

"That woman is exasperating!" Cora scrunched up her nose and squeezed her eyes shut as Conrad chuckled.

"Do you have your tickets for the show?"

"Of course, I do, for both of us. Center aisle, fifth row. Right where I like to sit."

"Well, then," Conrad held his hands out. "We'll find out then."

"That's not the point and you know it!"

Conrad swallowed his laughter. "Here comes Peggy. She's coming down the aisle."

Cora turned in her seat to stop her. "You have the dress done?"

"I do. Hi Chief."

Conrad nodded his hello.

Cora lifted the plastic and looked at the bottom of the dress. Peggy had cleaned it and tucked the bottom ruffle up to hem it. She removed the ruffles on the bodice and replaced it with blue satin ribbon. "It's lovely."

"Thank you."

"Is that my dress?" Nina walked up and peeked under the plastic. "I love it! I can even wear that after the play is over!"

"I'm glad you like it." Peggy pulled the

plastic down.

“Oh, I’m Nina Arnett.” Nina looked at Cora Mae. “I’m playing Fiona Starkweather.”

“I’m Cora Mae Bingham and this is Conrad Harris. It’s nice to meet you, Nina. Have you acted before?”

“No, not really. I mean, I did some skits in high school, but they were just for fun. This is really exciting and scary at the same time.”

“Do you know what part Harvey Salzman is playing? Saucy?” Cora Mae pointed toward the front row as Conrad elbowed her.

“Oh, him. Yeah, he’s the director.” Nina nodded and reached for the dress. “I’m going to take this backstage. Should I try it on just to be sure it fits?”

“That would be a good idea.” Peggy nodded as Nina rushed down the aisle with the dress bag in her arms.

“Good try.” Conrad turned to his side when Peggy sat down behind them. “I don’t think what Saucy is doing down there is directing.”

"She must not know who he is." Cora Mae shook her head in confusion. "She should know that Eleanor is directing, though. I don't know what to take from that."

"My suggestion would be—."

Cora Mae interrupted him with her imitation of his canned response. "Wait until the opening night. Yeah, I know."

Conrad and Peggy laughed as Cora Mae rolled her eyes with a smile.

"You two are cracking me up tonight." Peggy smiled.

"I think I'm getting on her last nerve this evening." Conrad's sheepish grin made Cora smile.

Cora Mae turned around in her seat. "Have you had any luck finding more dresses?"

"No. I went out to the school and Danny Wittig let me look around. Nothing. I tried to talk to her son, Doug, and he was barely civil. I didn't even ask about the dresses. The young man is extremely difficult to chat with. Tomorrow, I'm going to try approaching Marty.

He's working out at Cajun's Motors, so I'm going to fake a car shopping trip. Wanna come?"

Conrad turned around in his seat. "I might. What time are you going out there?"

Peggy leaned back in surprise. "Mid-morning, probably. I need to wait for Arlene to cover for me. Are you wanting to talk to Marty, too?"

"I'd like to hear what he has to say about the accident. I've got a few questions about it. I won't interfere in your dress hunt. I'll just tag along as a helpful friend, if you don't mind."

"I don't mind at all! You think there's something fishy about that accident?" Peggy could tell he didn't want to answer. "Most of us thought the same thing. Olive would not have been driving out Rosemary Road at eleven o'clock at night with her boys at home unless something was going on."

"I have a lot of unanswered questions. I thought he might have some insight, but I didn't want to come at him with a police investigation.

I want the setting to be an informal inquiry. I think we have a better chance of getting somewhere that way."

"Same as me! I don't want to buy a new car, so I'm going to trap him in a test drive, so I can find out what he knows!"

Cora Mae laughed. "I like the way you think, Peggy."

# Chapter 15

Conrad pulled up in front of the Carom Seed Craft Corner in his personal vehicle and waited for Peggy. He had on slacks and a shirt today, no uniform. It had caused some upset at the station that morning and at the bakery when he met his breakfast buddies for coffee, but it seemed like the right way to handle this setting. No one believed him when he said he was taking the day off, though, because he'd never done that before.

Peggy jumped into the passenger seat and rubbed her hands together nervously. "You look nice today."

"Thank you."

"Not that you don't look nice in uniform." Peggy tittered nervously. "I'm just not used to seeing you in regular clothes."

"Well, I'm not used to being in them much, but I thought it best for this outing."

"You're probably right."

Conrad turned the heat up in the car. He couldn't tell if she was nervous or cold, but she was fidgeting. "Do you know how you want to handle this?"

"Not really. It depends on how he reacts, I guess. I've been warned that he has a temper, so I'm going to tread lightly and lean on the friendship with his mother as my angle."

"Sounds good. We'll play it by ear. What kind of car are you looking for?"

Peggy cocked her head at Conrad with a quizzical look.

"You need a story for why we're here!" Conrad was beginning to think his sidekick was not ready for this.

"Oh, yeah! I do. I want to keep my old

truck for events, but I need a small economical car for everyday use."

"Do you have a price range?"

"Six thousand? Does that sound okay?" Peggy hadn't thought about price and hadn't purchased a car in a decade, so she really didn't know what the current rates were.

"That's okay. They should have something, but it will have a lot of miles on it."

"I see him." Peggy pointed to the far side of the lot. "He's taping a tag on a window."

"I'll park on that side, so maybe he'll come to us. I'd rather not have Ella see us first or she'll want to take over."

Getting out of the car quickly, Peggy waved when Marty looked their way.

"Can I help you?" Marty walked toward the two and sudden recognition crossed his face. "Chief Harris."

"Just Conrad today." Conrad stretched out his hand to shake. Although they hadn't formally met before, everyone knew Conrad on sight. "I'm tagging along on my day off to help

Peggy car shop."

"Hi, Marty. You may not remember me, but I'm Peggy Cochran and I own the craft store in Spicetown. I was a friend of your mother's and involved a lot with her plays at the school."

"Nice to meet you. What kind of car shopping are we doing today? Can you tell me what you're looking for and I'll see if I can *steer* you in the right direction?" Marty laughed at his own play on words.

Conrad thought his joke rather brave, considering his recent steering damaged two cars on the lot. "She's not trading in anything. She's looking for a small car to run around town in. Nothing fancy. Good gas mileage."

"I've got just the thing. Follow me." Marty led them across the lot near the entrance to two small shiny sedans, one black and one blue. "Both of these beauties will get you thirty miles to the gallon."

Peggy walked around and looked at the sticker price. "This is more than I'm looking to pay."

"Okay, what's your price range?"

"I'd like to stay under six thousand."

Marty hummed. "Well, that narrows your options, but I do have one that might work. Follow me." Marty walked over to the far side of the lot where cars were arranged a bit haphazardly, as if they were awaiting repair. "This is an older car, but it has a clean record. No accidents and only one owner. Do you want to take a look at it?"

Peggy nodded.

"I'll get the keys." Marty jogged back to the store and Peggy peered in the windows.

"This is all you get for six thousand dollars nowadays? My truck better run forever!"

Conrad chuckled.

"How can teenagers ever save up to get their first car?"

"They don't," Conrad said. "Their parents buy them one."

Peggy nodded. "I see him in there talking to Ella. Do you think she'll come out here?"

"I hope not. Hopefully, he'll tell her that

it's you that's shopping, not me. If he uses the mother angle, she might stay clear of it. I don't think she trusts him yet, and she'll try to take over the sale. It's not fair to him, though. He needs a chance to try to prove he can sell a car."

"Well, now you're making me feel bad." Peggy put her hands on her hips. "We both know he's going to fail with me."

Conrad laughed.

"You know the whole town is going to think we are dating now, don't you?"

"What? Why is that?"

"Because of Ella! She sees you out here helping me in plain clothes! She goes to the beauty shop just like the rest of us."

"Speak for yourself there. I've never stepped foot in the place."

"Well, I can assure you that once Louise Morgan gets a hold of this hot story, it will spread like wildfire!"

"I guess after we fake buying a car, we can fake breaking up then." Conrad laughed at the absurdity of the Spicetown gossip mill.

"Another story I've got to create. My imagination is already taxed."

"Here we go. Let's get these doors open and you can take a look." Marty held the driver's door open and invited Peggy to take a seat. "What do you think?"

"Can we take it for a test drive?" Peggy looked up at Marty.

"Sure. I just need to make a copy of your driver's license."

Peggy pulled her purse around to her lap to get it out and handed it to Marty.

"I'll be right back." Marty jogged off again and Peggy got out of the car.

"So, do you want to start, or should I?"

"You start. You've already got the foundation of your friendship with Olive to launch off. Then just mention that you made some costumes and tell him about the girl with the blue dress. That will get you to a place where you can ask what you want to know."

"You're very good at this!"

"Thank you. It's kind of what I do."

"I've never thought of it that way, though."

"You think I just go around arresting people?" Conrad grinned.

"No, but I don't know, I just think you right wrongs, I guess. It's hard to explain, but I never thought about how much you have to talk to people and get them to tell you stuff."

"Pretty much every day."

"I can see that now."

"We're all ready." Marty handed Peggy her license. "Chief, I'll get in the back so you can sit up front."

"Thank you." Conrad sighed with relief. He wasn't sure his body shape was made for a compact car backseat. Just navigating the tiny opening behind the front seat alone would take acrobatic skills he had never had.

Marty slid himself under the seatbelt and turned his knees to the side. "There's not much passenger space in the backseat. Will that be a problem for you?"

"Oh, no. I'm not one to travel in a group. In fact, having a small car means someone else will always want to drive. It saves me gas!" Peggy smiled. "All ready?" Adjusting the rear-view mirror, she backed the car from the space and drove onto the highway, headed toward Red River.

"You know, Marty, I used to make costumes for the high school plays. I sew a lot and do alterations." Peggy looked in the rear-view mirror, and Marty nodded. "The funniest thing happened recently. They are working on a new play right now, and a young woman who is in the play, brought me a dress that she wanted me to alter for her role. Well, it turns out that I made that very dress twenty-five years ago for one of your mother's plays at the high school. Can you believe that?"

"Yeah, she really enjoyed those productions."

"This girl couldn't tell me where she got the dress. Her sister found it somewhere, I guess it was a second-hand shop. Do you know what happened to all of those costumes your mother had? I know the community center could sure use them for all the community plays. Every play we have, we scramble to find costumes for the roles."

"No, I figured the school had them."

"They've looked for them and found nothing. I assumed she kept them at home back then."

"Uh, yeah, now that you say that I think they were in the hall closet when I was growing up."

"Do you think your dad still has them?" Peggy raised her eyebrows and looked in the mirror, immediately seeing she had said the wrong thing by his expression.

"Not my dad. My dad is Billy Nash. Ralph Vogel might still have them. I wouldn't know about that."

"How is Ralph?" Conrad asked, even though he didn't know the man. He tried to turn in his seat to see Marty's face but didn't have the shoulder room. He wished he'd been limber enough to fit in the backseat so he could have kept a better eye on him.

"Okay, I guess. We don't keep in touch."

"Is your dad doing well? I haven't seen him in a while." Peggy turned to Conrad. "His dad used to work on my last old car all the time. He worked down at Wade's back then."

"He's doing okay. How does the car feel? Do you like it?"

"Can I turn around up here at the mobile home lot?" Peggy turned the blinker on to pull into a mobile home sales business that had a small gravel entrance. Glancing at Conrad, she said, "I think it's your turn now. Do you want to drive back? We can switch places here."

"Sure." Conrad nodded his understanding. Peggy had the information she came for and it was his turn in the rear-view mirror. "You don't mind, do you Marty?"

"Not at all, Chief! You have to drive a car to really check it out."

After seats were switched and seatbelts clicked, Conrad pulled the car back onto the road to return to the car lot. "I was planning to go visit Ralph Vogel. Is he still living in the same place?"

"As far as I know. Like I said, we don't keep in touch."

"I recently got a bunch of files sent over to me from the county sheriff's office. We always share information when we both answer the same call, and your mom's accident was one of those files."

"Really? That was over twenty years ago!"

"I know, but everything is getting scanned nowadays to digital to preserve records, so we are giving it all a look-over to get things in order before closing them up."

Marty nodded. "Makes sense."

"That was before my time, you know. I wasn't living in this area back then and didn't get a chance to meet your mom, but I've heard nothing but great things about her."

"Yeah, she was pretty awesome." Marty's smile was wistful and the conversation did not seem to be agitating him.

"I looked at that report they gave me, and I had so many questions. There seems to be a lot of detail missing, so I'm going to try to gather up some answers before I close it. You were old enough at the time. You might be able to give me what I need and save me a visit to Ralph."

"I'm happy to help if I can."

"That would be great. I know we can't really do this here. Do you have some time to come by the station or would you rather I come by your house? I don't want to interfere with your work. I'd have Ella on my tail!" Conrad chuckled. "No one needs that."

Marty laughed. "I start at ten tomorrow, so I can come by the station in the morning before work, if that's okay."

Conrad pulled the car into the lot and parked it. "That'll be fine. I'll be there by eight."

After Marty pulled himself from the back seat, he locked the car doors and turned to Peggy. "So, what do you think?"

"I like it. It sounded good and was comfortable."

"We just started our hunt today though,"

Conrad walked around the car. “I want to look a few more places before we make a decision.”

“Oh, I understand perfectly. Here, take my card. Call me with any questions or come back and see me. I know I can get you a good deal!” Peggy put his business card in her purse and thanked him. “Have a good day!”

Once Peggy and Conrad returned to his car, Peggy was jittery with excitement and delighted the mission was over. “I’m so glad you came with me. I wouldn’t have made it through that alone.” Conrad had saved her several times when she couldn’t think of something to say.

“You did just fine, and you got the info you wanted. I know it doesn’t lead you to the costumes, but it gives you some direction. He clearly doesn’t have them.”

“And he was putty in your hands! You got just what you wanted. He’s coming to your office to tell you everything he knows. That was amazing!”

Conrad laughed.

"Whew, I'm so glad that's over." Peggy sighed.

Sheri Richey

# Chapter 16

That afternoon, it was Peggy's turn to watch the puppy because Arlene had an appointment. "There you are!" Peggy smiled when Arlene walked through the door of the Carom Seed Craft Corner. "I was beginning to get worried."

"I'm so sorry. I never thought it would take this long! One thing just led to another. I was late getting there. I thought I knew my way around Paxton pretty well, but this attorney's office was tucked away in the old part of the downtown over a store. Thank you for watching little Wrinkles for me."

"Wrinkles? You named him?" Peggy

looked at the crate and back at Arlene.

"Don't you like that name? That was Dorothy's suggestion."

"You're going to have that little spud so confused that he'll never learn his name!" Peggy laughed.

"Spud! I kind of like that." Arlene waved the thought away. "Anyway, I was a little late for my appointment."

"But did you like him? Ned Carey doesn't recommend too many people."

"I did. He's an older man and only does real estate law. Nothing else. He has a part-time secretary, and it's just him. Maybe the practice was bigger in the past. I think he might be semi-retired. You know, the ones that can't quit completely."

Peggy nodded. "So, have you decided to accept Mavis' offer to buy the farm property?"

"I have. We have to talk about some road easements though, but it's just a formality. I can't believe Mavis wants to take this all on. She is not a young woman anymore."

"She doesn't know that." Peggy smiled. "I think she's enjoying this new plant adventure and maybe she's trying to help her son find his way. He's bounced around to different jobs and hasn't found a future. I think maybe she wants to create something she can pass on to him."

"That's a nice thought, but I can't help but think she's taking on too much work for herself. She's all alone out there!" Arlene shook her head. "What if something happens and she can't handle it? All of her money from her husband's life insurance will be tied up in land she might have a hard time selling."

"I'm sure she's thought this through. Mavis isn't flighty, and she's got Danny to step in if needed. She's trying to talk him into moving back into the house with her. He took an apartment in Paxton because he was working over there, but the cost of commuting is less than the apartment rent. I guarantee you she's got a plan."

"I hope you're right. Well, I guess I need to run Rover to Shelby's house. She said he could spend the night there. Are you ready to lock up for the night?"

"I am. I was just waiting for you. I'm running over across the street to the community center if you want to go along." Peggy pointed out the front window.

"Did you do another alteration?"

"No, I just thought I'd look for Eleanor and ask her about the costumes. I know Cora warned against it, but I'm running out of ideas. The only thing left is asking Ralph, and I really don't want to do that. I'm going to take a risk and see what Eleanor has to say."

"Okay. I'll go with you if you think it's okay to take the pup inside."

"Oh, I'm sure they won't care. You might even find someone interested in him. Does Eleanor like dogs?"

Arlene sneered. "I don't think Eleanor likes anything."

Peggy laughed. "Come on. Let's give it a shot."

---

Walking down the auditorium aisle, Peggy and Arlene stopped when Nina approached them. "What a cutie!" Nina Arnett scratched the puppy's ear. "What's his name?"

"He doesn't have one yet." Arlene stroked her hand down the dog's back protectively.

"He looks like a Skippy to me."

Peggy looked at Arlene. "Did you meet Nina when she came over for her fitting? This is Nina Arnett."

"I didn't. Hi, Nina. I'm Arlene. You had the blue dress?"

"Yeah. Oh, this is my sister Hannah." The small girl with long blond hair walked up behind Nina and smiled. "This is the lady that made that dress you gave me."

"Oh, hi. It looks really nice since you fixed it up." Hannah put her finger under the puppy's nose and the puppy began to gnaw on it.

"Where did you get that? I'd love to check

and see if there are more like it," Peggy said.

"My boyfriend had it. I think it was his mom's. She's dead now, though." Hannah wiped her wet hand on her jeans.

"Ew!" Nina recoiled. "You gave me a dead woman's dress?"

"She didn't die in it or anything!" Hannah rolled her eyes.

"Still!" Nina scowled.

"The lady I made the dress for died in a car accident over 20 years ago. It sounds like maybe you got this from Doug Vogel?" Peggy raised an eyebrow.

"Yeah!" Hannah nodded. "He gave it to me when I told him about the play. I think he meant for me to wear it, but my role is Paula Thompson and she's a southern belle, so I have to wear something frilly. Nina's part is the rich lady, so the dress will work better for her."

"Does Doug have other costumes from his mom? Maybe there's something in there for you, too?" Arlene shrugged.

"I haven't asked him. He thinks I'm

wearing that one, and I never told him I gave it to Nina. I'm not talking to him right now anyway, so..." Hannah looked away, miffed.

"You two have a fight?" Peggy smiled.

"He's impossible." Hannah rolled her eyes.

"Yes, men can be that way." Peggy nodded.

"I'm not worried about it. I think I found a dress I like in the ones Ms. Cline has backstage. I'll wear that if it's okay with her."

"Have you done this before?" Arlene tilted her head with interest. "Have you been in a play?"

"No. We just tried out because it sounded like fun. Doug's mom did them all the time, and I thought he'd do it with me, but he wouldn't try out, so I brought my sister. I guess we were pretty good since we both got picked!"

"Well, I'm sure you will both do well." Peggy smiled. "If you find out there are other costumes around somewhere, please let me know. I'd like to put them to good use."

"Sure thing!"

"Bye."

As the young girls headed toward the lobby, Peggy and Arlene found seats a few rows back from the stage.

"Do you really think they can pull this off?" Arlene whispered. "They don't seem very bright."

Peggy chuckled. "Cora Mae says that's just youth, but I thought the same thing. I guess all they have to do is memorize lines, and hopefully not too many."

Arlene's eyes widened, and she nodded in agreement. "She seems a bit young for Doug, or maybe he's just an old soul. How old would he be now?"

"He was thirteen when his mom died, so he's in his mid-thirties. He looks older than that, I think." Peggy pointed toward the stage. "I see Saucy in the front row. He's got a little dog. Maybe he would be interested in the pup. Let's move down there between scenes."

Once the scene ended and Eleanor's back

was turned, Peggy and Arlene slinked toward the front seats like ninjas. Eleanor would scold them if they were disruptive to practice, so great care was taken when pulling down the seat beside Saucy.

"Hey, ladies!" Saucy said in hushed tones.

"Hi, Saucy. How are you?"

"I'm good. Just enjoying the play. Jason Marks is really good in this one. What are you gals up to tonight?"

"I just came by to see if I could talk to Eleanor and Arlene came with me to show someone her pup."

Saucy sprang forward and looked around Peggy. "You got a new pup, Arlene?"

Arlene passed the puppy to Peggy to show Saucy and leaned forward. "No, we found him in the alley, and I'm trying to find him a good home."

"Isn't he a cute little bear cub!" Saucy held his hands out to take the pup from Peggy. "What's his name?"

"He doesn't have a name yet. Any

suggestions?" Arlene smiled.

"Hmm." Saucy held him up in the air with a hand under each arm. "Brutus or Roscoe. He looks like a tough guy, or he will be when he grows into all this skin." Saucy chuckled and then looked sheepishly at Eleanor. Kissing the puppy's face, he handed him back to Peggy.

"I'm afraid my little Zippy wouldn't stand for me bringing home another dog. She's the jealous kind." Saucy smiled. "I don't even think she likes other dogs. I have to keep them out of her sight, or she'll carry on like she's losing her mind."

"That's too bad." Peggy sat the pup in her lap. "I thought she might like a playmate."

Arlene leaned forward. "My Jet is the same way, so I can't keep him. Do you know anyone else that might be interested?"

"Not that I can think of right now." Saucy frowned. "What kind of dog is he? You think he'll get big?"

"Hymie Morgan said he thinks he's a bulldog mix. He might be stocky, but not tall."

"Hmm, I'll let you know if I think of anyone. I'll see Bert Miller in the morning, and I'll ask him."

"Thank you." Arlene saw Eleanor coming their way and sat back in her seat.

"Saucy, if you're done chitter-chattering over here, can you go backstage with Jimmy and help him with the props?"

"Yes, ma'am. I'll do that right now." Saucy said his goodbyes as he shuffled to the stage stairs.

"Eleanor, do you have a minute?" Peggy patted the seat beside her. "I just had a quick question."

"I suppose I've got a couple. They have to move some things for the next scene."

"Thanks."

"Hi, Eleanor." Arlene leaned forward. "The play looks like it will be wonderful, and I see you have some new faces in this one."

"Yes, we have some newcomers." Eleanor left her appraisal unsaid. "What do you have here?" Pointing to the puppy, Eleanor studied the dog's face. "Bulldog. Is it yours?"

"No," Peggy said. "Arlene found him in the alley, and she's trying to find a home for him."

"They drool a lot." Eleanor lifted her chin. "My father was fond of the breed."

"Would you be interested in the pup?" Peggy asked before Arlene could object.

"No. No, my lifestyle doesn't lend itself to pet ownership. I'm away from home far too much."

"Oh, okay. Well, what I wanted to ask you about is the costumes. I fixed the Arnett girl's dress, and she says it fits. That blue dress is one that I made for a high school play back when Olive Vogel was alive. Do you know what happened to the rest of her costumes? I made a number of different things for her and if we could find those old costumes, it would be easy to adapt them to whatever you needed for future plays."

"No, I've never found them at the school. I assumed she kept them secreted away somewhere and her family didn't see fit to give them to the drama department after she passed. You might ask that husband of hers about it, although I don't think he has a conscience. It's a shame he didn't donate those items back then, but he wouldn't even attend the plays when she directed them. Everyone else knew those plays were important to her, but he never acknowledged them at all."

"I don't know him, so I've been reluctant to try to contact him." Peggy bit her lip. It looked like that would be the only option left.

"Well, my experience was not pleasant, but it was many years ago. He was a bit of a ruffian back then, without an ounce of civility. However, he may have mellowed with age."

If Eleanor found him uncivil, he must be quite unruly. Peggy hummed. "Thank you, Eleanor. I'll let you know if I find them." She sure wasn't looking forward to meeting Ralph Vogel.

# Chapter 17

The next morning, Conrad glanced at the monitors in the dispatch cubicle that showed the parking lot. "That young man is coming to see me, Georgie."

"Okay, Chief."

"Marty! Good to see you." Conrad held up his hand in greeting. "I appreciate you giving me a bit of your time this morning. Let's go back to my office."

"Sure thing, Chief. Happy to help."

"Could you use some coffee? I can get you a cup."

"No thanks, Chief. I just had some before I left home."

"Take a seat there and if you don't mind giving me a minute, I haven't had my quota yet." Conrad chuckled as he warmed his coffee up.

Marty sat back in his chair, relaxed and smiling. Conrad hoped to keep him that way, unguarded.

"Let me tell you a little bit about what I got here." Conrad opened a file folder and gave Marty a look of concern. "I hope these pictures won't trouble you to take a look at. They are just pictures of the car."

"No, that's fine." Marty leaned forward to look.

"I've got a couple of pictures of the car, one before the tow and the other after. Maybe being a car guy like you are, you'll see right away what put a question to my mind, but—."

"The back wheel." Marty pointed at the picture. "Ralph already told me that the tire came off and caused the accident."

"Did he now!" Conrad cocked his head. "That sure isn't in any of the reports. I wonder why he was so sure of that."

"He wanted to blame me for it." Marty's jaw clinched, and Conrad saw he was losing that pleasant demeanor he had hoped to maintain.

"He holds you responsible for the wheel? How so?" Conrad scratched his chin.

"I put new tires on her car a couple of days before the accident, and Ralph says I didn't do it right."

"Was the night of the accident the first time anyone had driven on the new tires?"

"No. Ralph had driven the car a couple of times."

"Then why didn't he wreck?" Conrad held his hands out.

"I don't know."

"Do you have concerns that the accident happened because of your work with the new tires?"

"No. It used to haunt me day and night, but I know that's not true. I've always known that I didn't do anything wrong, but I couldn't handle Ralph and Doug blaming me. Now I don't let it eat at me anymore. I've learned to cut them out of my life and go forward. My wife, Sandy, taught me that, and it's the only way I've found any peace with them."

"That sounds like a healthy outlook." Conrad nodded. "The reason I brought it up was because the officers at the scene didn't even suspect that was the cause. Looking at the pictures, I did notice it, but I can't say what caused it. There could have been an animal run out in front of her car. People automatically swerve for animals even when they know it's not safe. It's instinct. The officers on scene thought it might have been a lingering ice patch on the curve. Nobody knows, so you are right to not let it eat at you."

Marty nodded and sighed. "Let me ask you something else. Do you know where Ralph was when the accident happened? I know you were home with Doug, but the reports don't confirm his location."

"Nancy's house." Marty shrugged. "I don't know that for sure, but it's what we all thought."

"Was Ralph having an affair with Nancy?"

"Yeah, and my mom knew about it. They'd fought about it, and we could hear them."

"When you say we, do you mean you and your brother, Doug?"

"Yeah. He knew about it, and it was beginning to cause problems between us, too. I have always hated Ralph since I can remember, but I didn't hold it against Doug. But when I found out Ralph wasn't treating my mom right, and Doug defended his dad, we just couldn't find any common middle ground anymore."

"You know he's moved back to Spicetown, right?" Conrad rocked back in his desk chair.

"Yeah, I've heard, but I haven't seen him."

"Will it be a problem when it happens? I mean, you're bound to see him at some point."

"Nah, we're strangers now. I'll just walk right past him, the same way I do Ralph. They don't exist to me anymore."

"I commend you for that!" Conrad leaned forward and his chair creaked. "It takes a big man to let things go. It's not easy."

Marty nodded shyly, unaccustomed to flattery.

"Do you remember why your mother left the house that night? Did she say anything to you about where she was going?"

"Yeah, she said she was going to see if she could find Ralph."

"She didn't say where she thought he was?" Conrad lifted an eyebrow.

"No, but I knew. I figured she was going by Nancy's, but she would never say that. She didn't talk to us boys about her marital issues."

"Did she seem angry when she left?"

"No, but she never showed that side, you know. She always had a cheerful face on everything, and she wouldn't want us boys to know if she was mad."

"Ralph told one of the officers that he was playing cards with a buddy. Did you ever hear that story?" Conrad tapped his pencil on the desktop. It irked him that the officer didn't collect the friend's name. That was a rookie mistake.

"No, but he never gave me any explanation."

"Do you recall him playing cards with friends back then? Was that something he did sometimes?"

"I think it was his excuse to not explain where he was going." Marty smirked.

"Do you remember who his friends were back then? I'd like to reach out and see if they remember that night. I don't find anything documented in the file to corroborate his story."

"The only one I remember is Pete Little. He worked with him, and he came by the house some. They used to go fishing once in a while on the weekends. Pete had a boat."

Conrad nodded. Pete was City Councilman Little's brother. He would be easy to reach. "Not to harp on a sensitive subject, but I have to ask, what makes you so sure that the new tires weren't the cause of the accident? I mean, the wheel is clearly off the car after the accident."

Marty dropped his clasped hands between

his legs and leaned forward on his forearms. "I was young, but I'd been doing work on cars since I was twelve. It's what my dad did for a living down at Wade's Garage. I spent every summer down there hanging out around him. This car was my mom's. I checked and double checked everything I did to it. I took it down to Wade's to get the tires balanced after I put them on. They would never have missed something like that. Those guys would have caught any mistake I could have made."

"The reports don't show any lug nuts found at the scene, but then again, I don't think anyone looked." Conrad shrugged in apology.

"I can't explain it, but I know I didn't leave them off."

Conrad nodded. "I wish I had something more to tell you, but I will let you know if I find out anything new."

"Thank you, Chief."

Conrad followed Marty to dispatch and said goodbye as he left the station. "Georgia, I need that high-powered magnifier we have around here somewhere."

"Is it getting hard on you to read nowadays, Chief?" Officer Eugene Tabor snickered.

Conrad scowled at him. "I've got a picture that the county sent over and I need to see the detail in it."

"Enlarge it." Tabor nodded.

"It's a paper photo from twenty years ago. It doesn't have fancy buttons to click. This is old school stuff." Conrad growled. Even he had grown fond of the digital world and the things Tabor could do for him.

"That's okay, Chief. I can scan it in, make it digital, pixelate it, and then we can enlarge it. It won't be perfect, but it can't hurt to try."

Conrad's head wobbled as he reared back from Tabor's description. "Okay. Go do all that slicing and dicing and then chop it up for dinner!"

Georgia laughed.

"Sure thing, Chief. Is it on your desk?"

Eugene got up from his desk and headed down the hallway to retrieve the photos.

"Yes, there are two of them. Both on my desk, but the best picture of the tire is the tow truck shot."

Tabor came back holding both photos. "What exactly are you looking for?"

"I want to know if there are any lug nuts in that back tire or on the wheel studs." Conrad tapped his finger on the photo. "The officers on the scene failed to notice and didn't look for lug nuts on the ground, either."

"They didn't notice the wheel was plum off?" Tabor's eyebrows came together as one.

Conrad chuckled. "I think they were just more concerned with the victim, and that distracted them from worrying about the cause of the accident. The reports are a little thin and I'm trying to fill in some gaps."

"I'll see what I can do." Eugene always liked a challenge.

# Chapter 18

"I'm sorry I'm late." Peggy called to Arlene when she came in the door. "I had to run by the library."

"No bother. I was here early to open." Arlene walked out of the storage room pushing a rolling cart of yarn skeins and hanks of pastel colored cotton.

"Where's little Sarge?" Peggy looked around the room. "The little Tootsie Roll pop munchkin."

Arlene smiled. "He's in the crate. He has a new toy to chew on that Shelby gave him."

"Did that go okay last night with him and all the other dogs?"

"She said it did. She said she could keep him tonight, too, but not Friday. Friday evening, she has plans to go to the play."

Peggy walked to the storage room entrance and gasped. "What did she do to him? Is he wearing clothes? He looks like a disgruntled leprechaun!"

Arlene choked on her laughter and walked back to the crate. "She gave me a harness for him, so I could leash train him. It helps to have that when he goes potty. The green band is called a belly band. It keeps him from tinkling in the house. She said even puppies that are potty trained sometimes tinkle when they get overexcited."

"Good gracious. How does he breathe with all that on him? I don't think green is his color."

"Oh, he's fine. It's just a little big on him." Arlene smiled. "Did you see Cece when you were at the library?"

"I did. I talked to her about helping us with the cross-stitch event the weekend after next."

"Is she free?" Arlene pushed the cart over to the far wall where the yarns were stored in cubbyhole shelving.

"Yes, and she said she would work with the children if any show up. She has some finished projects to bring for displays as well." Cece Fields, the manager at the Spicetown Library, was an avid stitcher, and her work was impeccable.

"Maybe we should include embroidery to broaden the options." Arlene pointed to the kits in the bin. "We could take those with us."

"We can. I don't have any finished projects to display, though. What are your plans today?"

"Nothing special. I talked to Mavis last night, and she's happy with the details. The attorney is going to send everything by mail, and we can get it signed and notarized at the bank."

"I have one little errand I'd like to run today." Peggy cringed.

"Are you really going over to Ralph Vogel's

house? What are you going to say?"

"I don't know yet." Peggy shook her head. "I don't know the guy. Maybe Nancy will answer the door. At least she should know who I am and that will smooth things out a little. It kind of depends on how he reacts."

"I don't think he's very friendly, and after meeting his son," Arlene pointed next door, "you may be headed into another really awkward conversation."

"I know." Peggy sighed. "At least Nancy is conversational. She never had any problems complaining about my stock or prices when she was in here, but I haven't seen her in a long time. She doesn't just stare numbly waiting for you to go away like..." Peggy pointed to Doug's barbershop.

"If there's nothing to complain about, she might be at a loss for words, though." Arlene chuckled.

"True." Peggy nodded.

"Don't you think it might be uncomfortable to bring up Olive to Nancy?"

"I hadn't thought about that, but it's been so long ago."

"Yeah, but if the town gossip is accurate, Nancy was involved way back then." Arlene's eyebrows raised.

"You may be right. She might be touchy when I bring it up." Peggy couldn't see any other way to do it. "I'm just going to take that chance. What's the worst that could happen?"

"They call the police on you for trespassing?" Arlene shrugged. "No wait, shooting at you to run you off the property! That's probably the worst."

Peggy laughed. "With that prediction, I think I'll return saying it didn't go so bad."

"That's the positive Peggy I was looking for!" Arlene laughed.

"I'll be right back." Peggy grabbed her purse from behind the counter.

"Yeah, I bet you will." Arlene raised her eyebrows and smiled. The encounter would probably take less than a minute total. "Good luck."

Nancy Whitehead's address was on the Carom Seed mailing list, so Peggy assumed that it was also the current residence for Ralph Vogel. She drove by the first time, intentionally missing it so she could get up her nerve, then circled the block to try again. Pulling up to the house, she turned into the driveway. There was no car parked outside, but the garage was shut, and she couldn't tell if anyone was at home from the street.

It was an older home on Lilac Drive with three front steps that led to a small concrete porch without a railing. The picture window had sheers, so she couldn't see in. Walking up the steps, she felt her heart pounding in her ribcage like raindrops on a tin roof. Timidly, she tapped on the door and jumped when the doorknob turned.

"Peggy!" Nancy Whitehead cocked her head to the left, then hesitated, at a loss for words. "How are you?"

"Hi Nancy. I'm well. I don't mean to

bother you, but I just stopped by to see if your husband might be home. Ralph?"

Nancy frowned. "No. He's gone fishing this morning with a friend."

Peggy looked down, debating about whether to leave Nancy with the question to pass on or the mystery to stew about. "Well, uh, I just had a quick question..."

"Come in!" Nancy opened the screen door and grabbed Peggy's upper arm. "I just heated some water for tea. Do you hear it?" Nancy rolled her eyes. "I need to get it off the stove. We can just both have a cup."

Peggy did hear the whistle of hot water and let herself be pulled through the front door. Once inside, Nancy ran to the right, and after looking around the living room, Peggy slowly followed. The furnishings were modest, a bit dated, but tidy. Too tidy to think someone lived here. There must be a family room in the back where real people relaxed.

"Sit. Sit." Nancy waved Peggy to the table. "Let me just get some cups. Is Earl Grey okay?"

Peggy nodded, although she was not a usual tea drinker. “You have a lovely home, Nancy.”

“Thank you!”

“I really didn’t mean to intrude.”

“Oh, nonsense. I’m not busy with anything. I’m just surprised to see you away from the store. Are you closed today?” Nancy poured hot water into each cup.

“No. I just had a few errands to run, and Arlene Emery is working this morning.”

“Oh, yes. I forgot Arlene worked there now. I saw her during the holidays.” Nancy placed a steaming cup in front of Peggy with a tea bag steeping in it. “Do you take sugar or milk in your tea?”

Peggy shook her head. She didn’t want to complicate things, and she didn’t want to drink the tea, but it seemed that wasn’t an option.

“So, now.” Nancy sighed. “What was the question you had?”

“Well, it may sound crazy, but I just wanted to ask. Years ago, I made a bunch of costumes for the high school students to use in their play productions. I hadn't really given it any thought in all these years until last week when one of those old costumes resurfaced."

"Really? Where was it?"

"A young lady brought it into the store to be altered. She has a role in the upcoming play at the community center. She said someone gave it to her for the role, but she didn't know where they got it."

"How surprising!"

"Yes, it was. I sew a little tag into everything I make, and I made this dress over twenty years ago."

"Wow!" Nancy's eyes widened. "How exciting to find it again."

"It was, but it made me recall that there were many costumes I made around this same time for the plays that were being done at the high school. I couldn't help but wonder what happened to them all."

"I can imagine." Nancy nodded.

"So, I went to the high school, and we

looked around for them, but they aren't there."

"That's unfortunate." Nancy stirred in a sugar cube and removed her tea bag from her cup.

Peggy imitated Nancy's movements and cleared her throat. "Yes, well, it was suggested to me that the costumes were probably at the Vogel home, rather than the school, so I wanted to see if Ralph could recall what happened to them."

"Oh! You mean you made them for Olive?" Nancy nodded her head. "I remember she did plays all the time."

Peggy nodded. She was relieved the issue was out there and Nancy had not seemed uneasy.

"I don't think they're here. In fact, I'm sure they couldn't be. I would have seen them." Nancy stared at the table between them for a moment in thought. "When I bought this house, Doug moved in here with me first and Ralph slowly moved his stuff in. He had a lot of furniture and clothing to get rid of at the old house, because I didn't have room here and he had to get that house ready for sale. I don't really know what he did with Olive's things."

"It was a long time ago." Peggy took a sip of her tea.

"Yes, it has been. I hope he remembers. I just thought he probably donated her clothing somewhere, but I don't recall him ever saying. Who told you she kept them at the house?"

Peggy racked her brain for an alternative to the truth but found none. "Marty said they were at home when he was a boy."

"Ah, Marty." Nancy smirked. "I'm surprised he would speculate, especially since he doesn't claim to even know Ralph when he runs into him. It's like neither of us exist!"

"Oh, he didn't say anything about you or Ralph. He just said the costumes were kept at home when he was a kid, rather than at the school. He didn't know what happened to them." Suddenly, Peggy felt fiercely protective of Marty. He had been kind when she had faked a test drive, and he hadn't spoken ill of Ralph or

Nancy. She wasn't going to tolerate Nancy doing that now. "I recently spoke with Doug, as well. You know he's setting up a store right beside mine."

"Oh, yes! I'm anxious to see it once he has everything ready. It's exciting to have him home."

"I'm sure it is. Where has he been living? I didn't think to ask him."

"Oh, he's been in several different places. I hope he's ready to settle down now and stays close. He has a girlfriend, so maybe grandchildren are not far off!" Nancy's smile beamed.

Peggy couldn't think of a diplomatic way to share the news of their tiff without it sounding tactless. "That's nice. Well, I need to get back to the store. If Ralph remembers anything, please let me know. The community center could really use those costumes and it would save me a lot of sewing!" Peggy chuckled and scooted her chair from the table to stand.

"Oh, I will. I'll ask him about it and let you

know if he can be of any help." Nancy followed Peggy to the door.

"Thanks for the tea and conversation." Just as Peggy pushed open the screen door, she saw a police car drive slowly by the house. "I'll see you soon."

# Chapter 19

"It's Peggy Cochran, Chief." Georgia confirmed Conrad's suspicion, but he had to run the plates to be certain.

"Thanks, Georgie." Conrad looped around the block slowly, stopping at the corner to look down Lilac Lane. When Peggy backed out of the driveway, she drove right by him at the intersection, and he followed her back downtown.

Parking in front of the Fennel Street Bakery, Conrad crossed the street and entered the Carom Seed Craft Corner store. He knew Peggy would be parking in the back, and it would take her a few more minutes to get inside.

"Hi, Chief!" Arlene tossed her hands up. "I don't think I've ever seen you in here before."

Conrad looked around the store in wonder. He had no idea what anything was. They just seemed to be selling colorful things. "I don't believe I ever have been." Conrad chuckled. "How are you, Arlene?"

"I'm doing great, Chief. What brings you down here today?" Arlene held up a finger. "Or am I in trouble? Did I do something wrong? Am I parked near a hydrant?" Arlene peered out the front windows.

"No, no. You haven't done anything wrong. I've just stopped by to check in with Peggy."

"Oh, I'm sorry, Chief. Peggy is out right now."

"She's coming." Conrad nodded toward the back room. "I saw her pull around back."

"Uh oh, is she the one in trouble?" Arlene feigned shock just as Peggy walked through the storage room door.

"Does that dog have on clothes?" Conrad scowled in obvious disapproval. "He looks like he's getting ready to jump from a plane."

Peggy laughed and pointed at Arlene. "I told you. It's not right."

"Shelby kept him last night, and she thought these things would be helpful."

"She might be over thinking it." Conrad growled. "Unless he's looking for work at the circus."

Still laughing, Peggy shook her head as Arlene opened the door to the crate. "Come here, Oscar." Arlene unfastened the green band around his body before picking him up. "Let's go potty." Turning back at the two still laughing, Arlene pouted. "You shouldn't tease a poor homeless puppy!"

"Oscar?" Shrugging, Peggy dismissed it as just another unsuccessful naming attempt. "So, Chief, are you stalking me? Was that you outside Nancy's house?"

"It was. I was planning to pay Ralph a visit and you beat me to it. I thought I better hear what you found out before I go give it a try."

"Ralph isn't home. She said he went fishing with a friend. I assume she means the bait and tackle kind of fishing, but it could be a new spin on playing cards with the guys."

"I'm glad I didn't bother stopping." Conrad preferred not to tip his hand. Fully thought-out answers were not usually as revealing as the ones you could get when the question was a surprise.

"I asked her about my costumes, and she said they'd never been in her house. She didn't know what he did with them, but she said he had to get rid of a lot of stuff before moving in with her. She didn't know what he did with Olive's belongings."

"Was she friendly and relaxed about your questions?" Conrad's forehead creased. Affairs of the heart could make things tricky. People did irrational things when love triangles were involved.

"She was. She said Doug moved in with her first and Ralph worked on the house to get rid of excess furniture and clothing before moving in."

"No mention of Marty?" Conrad scratched his chin.

"She asked me why I thought Ralph had the costumes and I told her Marty said they were in his house when he was a boy. She jumped on that and tried to twist it to mean Marty said Ralph had them. I corrected her, but she clearly doesn't like Marty. She said he won't even speak to them if he sees them."

"He pretty much said the same thing to me this morning. He came by the station and told me that Doug and Ralph blame him for Olive's accident because he put new tires on her car the week before the accident."

"Oh, no. Do you think that caused it?" Peggy placed her palm over her heart. That would surely tear a family apart.

"I don't think so because he said Ralph drove it a few times after he put them on."

"People always look for somewhere to place the blame. I guess it gives them closure."

Conrad nodded. “Well, you have a nice day.”

“Bye, Chief!” Arlene called from the back as she returned with the pup.

“You, too.” Peggy reached out for the puppy as the bells on the door clanged when it closed. “No more swaddling clothes for you. It’s time to be a man.”

“Oh, he is,” Arlene smiled. “He pee-peed outside like a big boy just now.”

Peggy covered both eyes with her hand. There was no end to humiliating this poor dog.

“I take it you didn’t find the costumes?”

“Nope, and I’m out of ideas. Nancy said they weren’t in her house, but she’ll ask Ralph if he knows what happened to them. I don’t hold out much hope for that. I guess they are lost forever.”

“Did you ask Doug?”

“I didn’t.” Peggy shrugged. “He just wouldn’t communicate, and I couldn’t seem to get the conversation going enough to go there. I should have, but I don’t think he would have told me even if he knew."

"I think you need to work on Hannah. She obviously has figured out how to talk to him if they're dating."

"I'm not sure they still are." Peggy leaned against the fabric table and the puppy squirmed to be released to run. "Hold him for a second." Peggy handed the pup to Arlene and went to the storage room. She walked out with a large jingle bell and a twisty bread tie. Fastening the bell to the back of his harness with a few quick twists, she took the pup and set him on the floor.

Pointing her finger sternly, Peggy glowered at the puppy. "Behave!"

"I did talk to Olive's best friend, Marsha Kent, when I was at the high school." Peggy spun around and looked up. "Did I tell you that? I should probably tell the Chief about that, too."

"Did that help?" Arlene's eyes followed the jingling puppy in fear he might chew on something. The store had a lot of low hanging items.

"She said Olive confided in her about her difficulties with Ralph. Marsha didn't know how Ralph disposed of her personal items, though. She did think Olive was probably going out to Nancy's house that night because she was worried about the rumors of Nancy's pregnancy, but they may not have been true."

"I can't think of any other explanation for Olive to be on that road at that hour." Arlene rushed over to the spinning rack of buttons. "No, no, no. We don't eat buttons."

"The bell is clearly not going to be enough."

---

"These are great, Tabor." Conrad looked through the prints that Eugene had enlarged.

"I know you didn't ask for this one," Eugene pointed to a photo on Conrad's desk. "But the county file had more pictures of the car taken back at the garage after the tow, and this one shows a lot of scratches underneath."

"So, what does it look like to you? Obviously, the axle is intact." Conrad was not a mechanic, but he knew the basics of a motor vehicle. The cause of this accident seemed directly related to the car and not the driver.

"Yeah. It looks like the wheel came off, but the undercarriage shows it didn't happen after the accident or as a result of hitting the concrete supports. The wheel happened first." Eugene looked hesitantly at Conrad. "At least that's what it looks like to me."

"I know a lot can go wrong, but without the car or a detailed report, I'm not sure how we will ever know what happened that night."

"No witnesses?"

"No. There's not a house in view of the overpass on the curve." Conrad hummed. "Who towed it?"

Eugene flipped through the papers spread across the desktop looking for a billing notice.

"Better yet where was it towed to? Someplace in Paxton?" Conrad pointed at the desk. “I wonder if someone at the garage looked at it or bought it for scrap. Maybe the tow driver or somebody at the garage remembers it.”

“Hmm.” Eugene looked up and smiled. “Wade’s Garage.”

“Well, I’ll be.” Conrad snickered. “I guess I know where I’m headed next.”

# Chapter 20

As Peggy reached above her front store window to pull down the pastel border decoration, she heard a door slam, and Hannah Arnett rushed out of the barbershop. Looking over her shoulder, she saw Arlene looking back. She had heard the door slam, too. Sharing a knowing look, Peggy backed down the step stool as Arlene approached.

"This might be a good time to try Doug again. It's a vulnerable time, he's distracted, and I bet that front door is still unlocked. Wish me luck!" Peggy flew out the front door before Arlene could voice any objection. Over-thinking things made her question her actions, so this time she was going to act on her instincts. She'd been turning their earlier conversation over in her mind all night and wasn't satisfied with how it went.

Peggy reached for the barbershop door and the knob turned. "Good morning, Doug. I'm sorry to interrupt you, but it will only take a minute."

Doug was installing a shelf under the counter on the wall and glared over his shoulder. Peggy ignored his scowl.

"It's customary here in Spicetown for business owners to support each other. You know, we have a merchant's association that Frank and Dorothy Parish run. They're the owners of the Caraway Cafe. Anyway, I thought since I'm next door to you, I should take the lead for the association and coordinate your opening with you. I know you don't have a date yet, and that's okay. I just wanted to give you a heads-up that we are all here for you, and I'll introduce you around at the next association meeting."

Doug stood up and turned. "Thanks, but I'm not interested in all that."

"I was over at your dad's house this morning and Nancy is really excited about your opening. She's excited that you've moved back to Spicetown, too. She said you've lived in all these different places, but we all hope you'll make this your permanent home."

"I've got a lot to do." Doug turned away, dismissing Peggy again, and she moved around to his side.

"One more thing I forgot to tell you the last time I was here, but I do the costumes for the community center plays, much like I used to do the ones for your mom at the high school years ago. Recently, one of the cast members brought me a dress to alter for the next production, and I discovered that it was a dress I actually made for your mom over twenty years ago! Imagine my surprise! Anyway, it got me to thinking about all those costumes your mother had. There were some military uniforms, a maid's outfit, lots of long dresses and suit coats. The community center could sure use those costumes now if they are still around. That's why I went by your dad's house this morning. Do you know where those costumes are stored now?"

Doug stood up and turned an angry glare on Peggy. Clinching a screwdriver in his right hand, his eyebrows pinched together, and he squared his shoulders. "Who brought you a dress to alter?"

"Nina. Nina Arnett. Do you know her?" Peggy was babbling nervously. "She's a cute young girl who says she lives west of town toward Red River. She's never acted before, but she's excited about the play and—."

"What does this dress look like?" Doug interrupted, seemingly unaffected by Peggy's anxious small talk.

"It's blue. Blue chiffon with a soft white ruffle around the neck and at the bottom, although I tucked the bottom of it up, because she wanted the dress shortened. I had to take it in at the waist a little, too."

Doug's face darkened. "Where is the dress now?"

"I took it back to the community center, so I'm sure it's backstage with the other costumes. I only had it for a day or two. It really didn't take much work. I'm not sure where it's been, but I had it cleaned after I altered it just to freshen it up. It was in good shape, though."

"Where did Nina get it?"

"I believe she said her sister got it for her, but she didn't say where. It might have been at a thrift store. That's when I remembered there were many more dresses that may be out there somewhere, and we could sure use them for the plays. It's not like they are being used as everyday clothing by someone, and it would sure save me a lot of work. It's easier to alter—."

Doug interrupted again, tossing his angry stare toward the front window. "That dress doesn't belong to Nina, and she didn't have any right to have it altered."

Peggy realized she was holding her breath and her bravado had run out. “I’m sorry. She seemed to feel that it had been gifted to her. I don’t think she meant....”

“It wasn’t.” Doug slammed the screwdriver down on the counter. “Can you put it back the way it was?”

“The alterations? Sure, I only tack in those stitches so I can always remove them for the next person needing the costume. Making these things adjustable is important when you need to reuse them all the time. Once the play is over, assuming she donates the costume back, I’ll return it to the way it was. Most people do donate their costumes because unless you want to wear them on Halloween...”

“It’s not hers to donate. It belonged to my mother, and I loaned it to Nina’s sister to wear for the play. I did not give it away. I would like it restored to the original and returned to me now.”

“Well, I’m not in charge of anything over there. I’m just a volunteer seamstress. The director is Eleanor Cline. You could go over to the practice tonight and talk with her or maybe just tell Nina's sister to get it back for you. I'm happy to fix it if you bring it over."

Doug scowled and looked away in thought. Peggy was not going to do his dirty work for him. He was being petty and selfish. After a few seconds, Doug grunted consent and returned to his work on the shelving.

"So, you have all of your mother's costumes? Did you put them in storage?" Peggy backed toward the front door slowly, sensing the question may trigger his frustration again.

"I'm not interested in donating anything. I'll get the dress back, and I'll appreciate it if you can restore it."

"I am happy to do that for you. Can you do something for me?" Peggy stood solidly on both feet within reach of the front door and waited. She was not going to proceed if he did not acknowledge her question.

After several seconds of silence, Doug

stood up and raised his eyebrows in agitation, but not anger. “What? What do you want?”

“I’d like you to be civil to me.” Peggy returned his gaze with a pointed stare. “We share a wall, a sidewalk, and a town. I would like to be able to have a cordial relationship with my neighbor.” When Doug did not reply, Peggy reached for the doorknob. “Have a good day.”

Arlene rushed to the front of the store when Peggy walked in. With her heart still pounding, she relayed the whirlwind conversation to Arlene as her heart rate slowly returned to normal.

“It sounds like he may have the same anger issues that everybody says Marty deals with.” Arlene’s eyes were wide with admiration. “He sounds a little scary.”

“I was surprised at the anger.” Peggy shuddered. “I expected him to be upset, hurt maybe from his spat with Hannah. She seemed mad when she left, but I didn’t realize he would also be angry."

"Maybe you made him angry and not Hannah. It sounds like the dress set him off."

Peggy puzzled over the sequence of events. Was he mad at the beginning? "He seemed more irritated at my visit at first. You may be right. He didn't get really angry until I mentioned the dress."

Arlene nodded. "I wonder what that fight was about."

"Maybe Vicki would know. I think I'll text her about Hannah stomping out, and maybe she'll be able to find out for us." Peggy pulled her phone from her pocket and sent a text message to Vicki Garwin at the Fennel Street Bakery. Vicki stayed too busy in the mornings to call, but she might notice Hannah coming back from her morning break mad, even without the warning text. "We can give her a call after lunch if we don't hear anything back."

Arlene nodded.

Peggy pointed to the dog crate. "Where's wandering Wally?"

"Oh, my!" Arlene covered her mouth with her hand. "She had opened the door to release him from his pen when he barked and had gotten distracted by the neighbor drama. "I'll find him!"

Peggy moaned.

---

After securing a phone number for Nancy Whitehead from Amanda's search of water department records, Conrad decided to try phoning first. It was always more challenging to approach a couple, and after Peggy's report of her visit, he didn't want to get dragged into anything between the couple. Perhaps Nancy could get Ralph to come down to the station to talk with him one on one.

"Good morning. This is Chief Harris of the Spicetown Police Department. Is this Nancy?"

"Yes, yes, it is. Has something happened?"

Conrad heard the anxiety catch in her

voice, as if he was the grim reaper calling. "No, ma'am. Nothing has happened. Nothing to worry about at all. I was just trying to reach Ralph Vogel. I was told he is your husband. Is that correct?"

"Yes."

"Is he at home?"

"No, he's not."

"Will you be seeing him today?" Conrad tapped his pen on his desk.

"Yes, but I don't know what time. Do you want me to have him call you?"

"Well, I'd rather he come down to the police station if he would. Today before five o'clock would be best. Do you think he could do that?"

"Uh, I don't know. Can I ask what this is about?"

"If he can't come today, please ask him to call me so we can make arrangements to meet. My schedule is pretty flexible. Can you do that for me?"

"Sure, Chief. I'll tell him."

"Thank you." Conrad ended the call and rocked back in his chair, wondering if he had made a mistake giving Ralph notice. Sometimes heightened anxiety helped, unless strategy was being plotted, but with Marty the only source, he didn't think Ralph would know what was coming. The only thing on Conrad's agenda next was lunch.

# Chapter 21

Peggy walked into the Caraway Cafe and turned left to look at the table in front of the window. Cora Mae sat there calmly scrolling through her mobile phone.

"Are you waiting on the Chief?" Peggy pulled out a chair at Cora's table.

"I think he'll be along in a bit, but he gets tied up sometimes. Still costume hunting?" Cora smiled and waved when Conrad walked through the door.

"No," Peggy moved to the next chair so Conrad could sit. "Actually, I found out who has the costumes!"

"You did? That's wonderful! Do you need help moving them to the community center?"

"No, because we won't be getting them." Peggy held her palms up helplessly.

Conrad frowned. "Where are they?"

"My guess is a storage facility, but Doug Vogel has them all and he is not interested in donating anything! In fact, he wants the dress I altered returned to its original state immediately and given back to him. He was quite angry to discover what he loaned to Hannah Arnett was given to Nina and altered. He didn't approve that, and now he's fighting with Hannah anyway."

Cora Mae shook her head and rolled her eyes. "My head is spinning from all that drama!"

"I know, right?" Peggy slumped against the table and propped her chin in her hand. "That young man is troubled. We had a scary conversation this morning. I don't think I'll go back over there."

"He got mad at you?" Cora sat up straight

in her chair. "For asking about dresses?"

"He gets irritated when I say hello. It's going to be difficult for him to run a business with a personality like a trapped animal."

"Indeed, it will." Conrad nodded, wondering what cage the young man was in. "He won't allow the costumes to be used? Did he say why?"

"He said they belonged to his mother. That was his reason. They belonged to my mother, and I do not wish to donate them." Peggy imitated Doug's seething irritation. "He only loaned the one dress to Hannah, his girlfriend, because he expected her to wear it in the play. When she gave it to her sister, he lost it. I think they may have broken up this morning, but I'm waiting on Vicki to come over to the shop for lunch and see what she found out."

"I guess you didn't hear anything more from Nancy?" Conrad looked at Peggy and Peggy shook her head.

"Nancy!" Cora turned to Peggy. "Did you

talk to Nancy Whitehead?"

"I did. I went over to their house to ask Ralph, but he wasn't home. Nancy said she'd never seen the costumes and said she'd let me know if Ralph could remember what he did with them."

"Sounds like you have stirred everybody in town up." Cora Mae chuckled. "Amanda said her mother was talking about Doug's barbershop last night. That means the word has hit the beauty shop!"

Peggy laughed and saw three lunch boxes stacked in the order window. "Oh, I bet that's our order. I've got to get going. See you later."

Cora Mae waved and turned to Conrad. "Peggy also talked to Olive's best friend when she was out at the high school. She thought she might know what happened to Olive's personal items after the accident. She had a good idea there."

"And do you know who that is?" Conrad was listening. This might be a path he could pursue, not for costumes, but for family dynamic questions. Peggy had good instincts. She just needed to become more comfortable with her extraction techniques.

"Marsha Kent." Cora nodded. "Marsha teaches geography at the high school. She and Olive were new teachers together, and that bond carried over into their personal lives. She said someone in the family should know."

Conrad nodded, committing the name to memory as he placed his order for lunch.

---

When Peggy returned to the Carom Seed Craft Corner, Vicki was already seated in the back with Arlene, and Vicki had been updated on the morning encounter next door.

"You better be careful," Vicki warned Peggy with a scolding look. "That boy could be dangerous!"

"He is an angry one. That's for sure." Peggy peeked inside each box and passed the lunches out. "I don't think I'll go over there again. I left the ball in his court. I told him I'd help him with his grand opening, if he wanted me to, but he's going to need to come talk to me on his own two feet."

"You didn't tell me that!" Arlene tensed. "You're going to help him?"

"It was just part of my mindless babbling. I was a nervous wreck over there and I couldn't stop talking. I told him about the merchant's association and how we help each other.... Yada, yada. I'm sure he wasn't even listening to me. If he did straighten up and ask nicely, of course I would gladly help him open."

"So," Arlene slapped her knee. "Did Hannah tell you anything?"

"Wait! Let me get my drink." Peggy ran to the storage room and came back with a bottle of water. "Where is that mud-colored muskrat?"

Arlene smiled. "He's an elf on a shelf! He's back on his little secret spot by the computer desk."

Peggy nodded. "Okay, I'm ready."

"Well, first off, I appreciate the text. You

were right. She came back from break in a huff, so I waited a few minutes until we were alone in the back and asked her if something was bothering her."

"She said she had talked to her boyfriend during break, and he made her mad. Then she corrected herself and called him her ex-boyfriend. She said she wasn't going to waste her time with him anymore."

"She didn't name him?" Peggy dabbed at her mouth with a napkin.

"No, but I asked if she was talking about Doug Vogel, and she said she was. I told her I knew he was opening a business across the street. I said that I had known his mother, and she was a very sweet person."

Arlene nodded. "She looked a little like Hannah, don't you think?"

Peggy did see a resemblance. Olive had been fair skinned with light hair as Hannah was.

"Hannah said she'd heard all about Doug's mom. She said Doug talked about his mom a lot and she found it rather weird. I asked her if they'd had a fight and she said lately that was all they did."

Peggy pointed her finger at Arlene. "She did say they had a fight when we saw her at the community center, and it looked like they had another this morning."

"She seems rather detached." Vicki frowned. "I don't know how to explain it, but I get the impression she doesn't really care for him as a person, but there's some reason she wished she could make the relationship work. It reminds me of Connie Baldwin. Do you remember her?"

Arlene chuckled. "The gold digger with the big poofy hair?"

"Yes! She didn't really care about her target. She was after their money, or at least that's what it seemed to everyone else. Hannah acts like that. It's very superficial."

"I'm pretty sure Doug doesn't have money." Peggy hummed. "But there could be something he has, or maybe there's a reason she needs to be in a relationship with someone all the time. Some people are like that, especially when they're young."

"When you're young, dating a business owner might seem like a big deal. How old is Hannah?" Arlene remembered feeling like Hobart was a worldly man when she met him because he ran his own farm. She didn't know it meant he put every dime into it and didn't have a minute of time to call his own.

"She's 27." Vicki rolled her eyes. "She looks and acts much younger, though."

"Does Doug come over to the bakery to see her?" Peggy pointed as she talked. "You would think he'd want to pop over there in the mornings before he started banging away next door."

"I've only seen him in the bakery a few times, and I couldn't tell he was there for her."

Peggy held her finger up, remembering her conversation yesterday. "Did Arlene tell you that I talked to Nancy Whitehead?"

"No."

"She's all excited that Doug is dating someone. She's already planning grandchildren."

"Oh, well." Vicki shrugged. "He must be 35 now. I wonder if this is his first try at dating. He's not doing a great job of it so far. Hannah said she has to tell him to take her to dinner and ask him how she looks. She's exhausted just trying to make him act like a boyfriend."

"He's pretty shy," Arlene said.

"He's pretty weird," Peggy added. "It would be interesting to hear how they met. I can't see him starting up a conversation with anyone."

"That's what I mean about Hannah. She seems to be working really hard at all this and I can't figure out why. I don't see that the young man has anything special to offer. She can do better." Vicki nodded curtly. "And I told her so."

"You may have just lost your new assistant!" Peggy sighed. Vicki had suspected she was only working there to be near her boyfriend.

Vicki nodded in despair. “Maybe someday I’ll learn to keep my thoughts to myself, but it hasn’t happened today.”

Sheri Richey

# Chapter 22

Walking through the bays of Wade's Garage, the potent smell of gear oil and exhaust hung in the air. Conrad greeted the workers as he passed through to the back, looking for the owner.

"Hey there, Wade." Conrad walked into the grimy garage office that Wade Henry used to sort bills and charges. The room was not much bigger than the desk he sat behind, and everything, including Wade, had a greasy film covering it.

"Chief! How're ya?"

"Good." Conrad sat in the chair Wade pointed him toward. "I saw Marty Nash in here last week. Is he back working for you?"

"Nah, he's just doing somethin' for Miss Ella. He still works for her. I'm not sure if that's going to suit him, but he's givin' it a try."

"Was he a good mechanic for you?"

"Yep." Wade ran his fingers through his hair and leaned back in his chair. "His daddy was good, too. Billy had some trouble with drinking, but I never had no trouble with him at work."

"I thought Marty would be as good as Billy. I was surprised he left."

"He was as good, and if it don't work out down at Ella's, I hope he comes back. I think he left because some of the guys were giving him a hard time. Plus, you know Ella. She can talk a good game. She had him convinced she could make him a millionaire, and he had dollar signs in his eyes. I can't blame him for that. Ella's hard to overcome."

Conrad chuckled. "She is somethin' else."

"Yep. Well, what can I do fer you today?"

"Can I pick your brain?"

"Well," Wade chuckled. "Don't hit it too hard. It's likely to shatter on me."

Conrad smiled. "I'll take it easy." Pulling a few pictures from his manilla folder, he slid them on the desk in front of Wade. "What do you make of that?"

Wade wrinkled his nose, squinted his eyes and grabbed for his reading glasses before studying the enlarged photo. "Hmm, are ya wantin' this fixed?"

"I'm wondering about what you think happened to it. I don't have the car anymore, but these are closeup photos from an accident. It's all I have to go by, but I wondered if you had any idea what might have happened here." Conrad had asked Eugene Tabor to enlarge the photos and crop out any part of the image that would show the make or model. He didn't want Wade to know he was looking at a twenty-year-old accident. He wanted him to focus on possible causes for the wheel loss.

"Yer wheel fell off. Any lug nuts around?"

"Not that they found."

"This better not be any work coming from my shop!"

Conrad chuckled. "No. No, it's nothing like that. I've just got a lot of questions about the cause of the accident. Is it natural cause, accidental cause, or malicious tampering?"

"I don't think these here pictures are enough to make that call, but if I were a bettin' man, I'd say there's nothing natural about this. I'd rule that out first."

"That's what gives me pause." Conrad nodded.

"It's possible that a distraction or interruption can cause a man to forget to secure a wheel. It's pretty rare, but it can happen, especially in a busy shop."

"Did that wheel cause the accident? Would that make you lose control on a turn even if the wheel didn't roll out?"

"It could. It definitely would have pulled the car to the right. Do we know what the suspension looks like? The axle didn't break." Wade tapped the photo.

"That's all I have. The car hit a concrete embankment just to the right of the road. It was totaled."

"A case of bad timing." Wade pushed the photos back across the desk to Conrad. "If that tire had worked off on a straight stretch of road, the car undercarriage would have hit the road with a thud, but the driver could have steered to the right and pulled over."

Conrad nodded. "One more question, if I walked out to the parking lot right now and took out every lug nut on one of my tires, how long could I drive around on it before I noticed or before something happened?"

Wade leaned back in his chair. "Depends."

"On what?"

"On where you drove and how you drove." Wade cleared his throat with a raspy cough. "If you drove around town real nice-like and didn't make no fancy maneuvers, you could bum around for a few days. Now, you hit the interstate ramp and start zipping around, passing folks at eighty, you won't make it to the next exit."

"Makes sense." Conrad nodded. "Would I notice anything? Any sound or vibration?"

"Might," Wade nodded. "Some do. It depends on how much attention you pay."

"Would you testify in court about this if needed?" Conrad stood up.

"Sure." Wade tossed his reading glasses on the desk. "Did somebody die from this?"

"Yes."

Wade dropped his head. "I'll be there if you need me."

"Thank you, Wade. You have a good day."

---

"Morning, Chief." Officer Fred Rucker only worked the weekend dispatch day shift, so Conrad didn't see him very often, unless he worked on a Saturday. "Did you see the sun is finally shining out there?"

Conrad smiled. "Yeah, it's about time."

"Sure is! I'm glad the weather's looking up. Have you got appointments today?"

Conrad was in uniform rather than street clothes. "I do. I've got a couple of interviews planned. I'm not quite sure how the day will unfold."

"Well, I'd rather be busy than bored! I am going to be studying my lines. Tonight is the play opening and I've got more lines this time than usual."

"What's your part?"

"I'm the private detective." Fred brushed off his lapel. "I'm going to solve the whole thing."

"Well, I'll be! I've got tickets, so I'll keep my eye on you." Conrad chuckled. This show must be a comedy.

"Where's Briscoe?"

"Oh, he's with Officer Kimball. She's hiking today, and she took him along. She's taken him out there before and says he loves it. He probably does, but it's not something you're going to see me do anytime soon."

"That's good for him."

"She'll probably drop him back by this afternoon. Who's on day shift today?" Everyone rotated Saturdays on the schedule, but they bartered and traded them off all the time. Conrad could never tell who was going to show up.

"Reynolds is in the office, Tabor is on patrol, and Hudson comes on second shift."

Conrad nodded and then walked into the break room to get water for his coffeepot. He hadn't heard from Nancy Whitehead and wondered whether he should have Tabor drive by the house. Vogel might be trying to avoid him.

Pink slips on his desk from the night shift showed Ralph had called in and left a return phone number, but no message. As he poured the water into his coffee maker, he saw a note that Peggy had called. The coffee would have to wait.

Dialing her number, he pulled out the chair behind his desk and reached for his notepad. “Peggy? It’s Chief Harris. I got a message you called.”

“Yes! Hey, Chief. It may be nothing, but it just came to me last night that I hadn’t told you about talking to Marsha Kent out at the high school. She was a close friend to Olive, and I ran into her when I was out there looking for costumes. Has she called you?”

“No, but Cora mentioned her to me.”

“Well, she said something to me that day and it didn’t register at the time, but she said she picked up Olive for work the day she died. Olive didn’t drive the car that day because Ralph said he needed it for something. It may mean nothing, but— “

“No. No, that kind of detail is exactly what I’m looking for. I’m going to talk to Ralph today, so it helps to know that.”

“One more thing, Marsha reminded me that back then, there was a rumor in town that Nancy Whitehead was pregnant. Marsha thinks Olive wanted to talk to Nancy about it, not because she was jealous or anything, but because she wanted to warn Nancy that Ralph was not a good father. She said Olive had been trying to call Nancy that day, but Nancy wouldn't answer."

"Thanks."

---

Peggy and Arlene put the finishing touches on the new window display for spring and Arlene folded the step stool flat. "I need to flatten that dog crate and wrestle it into my car, because Margo needs it back for the weekend. Her daughter is coming over Sunday."

"But what are you going to do with the chocolate drop tonight?"

Arlene swallowed. "He has to go to the shelter." Arlene turned away and took the boxes back to the storage room.

"He's going to Shelby's tonight, right?" Peggy knew Arlene was about to cry.

Arlene shook her head, avoiding eye

contact. “She’s going to the play tonight.”

“Amanda has a cat carrier that she dropped off. It’s in the back room. We can keep an eye on him during the day here at the store. He’ll be fine.”

“I don’t have a plan for tonight, though. I don’t have any more plans at all. I’m all out of friends and he has nowhere left to go.” Arlene threw her hands up and Peggy saw her eyes were tearing.

“If we can’t find him a place for the night, I’ll take him home.”

Arlene’s chest heaved. “Really? Would you? Oh, thank you, Peggy. I just can’t dump him at the shelter. He’s already been dumped once, and he deserves something better than that.”

“It’s not a permanent solution, but I can handle a night, I think. Last resort only.”

Arlene nodded and whispered, “Okay.”

Sheri Richey

# Chapter 23

Conrad strolled out to the dispatch booth and looked at the parking lot cameras, waiting for Fred to finish an incoming phone call.

"Everything all right?" Conrad asked when he saw Fred writing a message on a pink slip of paper.

"Yeah. It's just some girl calling for Hudson. He needs an answering service. I think he must not answer his cell phone and these women all call to leave him messages up here. I get them every weekend."

Conrad chuckled. "Maybe he just needs to

pick one."

"I'm sure this is more fun." Fred gave an impish shrug. "What can I do for you, Chief?"

"Get Tabor on the radio and tell him to go by Ralph Vogel's house when he gets free. It's time to round him up. It's past ten o'clock and I'm not wasting my whole day on this."

Conrad looked in the break room and then waited until Fred finished relaying his message. "Where's Jennings? Did he go out?"

"He just ran to the bakery. He'll be right back."

"Tell him to look in the barbershop across the street and see if the owner is tinkering around in there. The place isn't open yet, but he's been working in there to get it ready, and you can usually see him through the front windows."

"He's out of the car right now, so I'll send him a text. I guess he's inside the bakery. Want him to get you something while he's there?"

"No, I'm good. Was that Tabor?" Conrad pointed at the radio. He heard a call come in, but it was muffled.

"Yeah, he's following Vogel in. They're headed this way."

Conrad nodded. That was for the best. He was just happy to hear he was home. He had thought he might try to run and then Conrad would have a hard time picking him up without any cause. He was pushing his luck as it was.

"Jennings said he doesn't see anyone in the barbershop. No lights on either."

Conrad walked down the hallway toward his office. He didn't have an address for Doug, but the city would have that information on the business license application. They wouldn't be open until Monday, though, and he hated to drag this out.

"Hey, Fred. Do you know if Cajun Motors is open on Saturday?"

"I believe so, Chief."

Conrad nodded. If Ralph didn't offer him some contact information, there was a chance that Marty might know where Doug was staying, if only to avoid him.

Conrad checked his phone and prepared a tall travel mug of coffee with some gingerbread creamer. He didn't know anything about Ralph Vogel and that always made an interview more challenging. He was going in blind.

Walking out to the lobby, Conrad leaned his elbow on the dispatch counter to await Vogel's arrival. Watching the camera monitor, he saw him roll out of the passenger side of a sedan as his wife stepped out of the driver's side door. Ralph Vogel was a large man, not just heavy, but well over six feet tall. He had a slow lumbering gait and rounded shoulders, but he came through the glass lobby doors with a grin and a boisterous bellow.

"Chief! So sorry I'm late! I'm Ralph Vogel and I know you wanted to talk with me today. So sorry to keep you waiting on me. I've got a bad back and some days it acts up on me. I was slow getting up and around this morning."

"Mr. Vogel," Conrad nodded his head and held his arm out. "We can go in here."

Ralph rocked from side to side as he

walked, almost limping without favoring one side or the other, needing the momentum to lift each foot to progress forward. He had gray hair that had been dyed brown, but not maintained, so there was a line of color change showing on the sides of his head. It took several minutes for Ralph to maneuver around the table in the interview room and become comfortable in a chair. Conrad stood with his foot in the seat of his chair, leaning his elbow near his knee, and waited.

"Now," Ralph panted, with a few beads of sweat glistening on his brow. "Again, I'm sorry for the delay. As you can see, I don't get around all that well anymore. I worked in construction for years and I'm paying the price for all that physical work now."

"I understand. I don't believe we've met before, but I'm Conrad Harris."

"Nice to meet you, Chief."

"Likewise. I've reached out to you today because I've got some questions about an old file we have. I don't mean to dredge up painful memories for you, but the accident file we have on your wife, Olive, is incomplete."

"Really? Was the information lost?" Ralph pulled out a handkerchief and dabbed at his forehead.

"I can't say. It all happened before I moved to town, but I have the county's file, as well as the city report, and there are a lot of unanswered questions here that I'm hoping you can fill in."

"Well, I'm sure happy to try. My memory is not what it once was though I'll warn ya." Ralph smiled and put his elbow up on the table.

"Where were you when the accident happened?" Conrad peered down at Ralph. He had remained standing for just this moment. If he had taken a seat, he would have been looking up at him. His long torso had him sitting higher in his chair than Conrad.

"I was at a friend's house. She knew I was planning to be out late. The guys from the job I was on liked to play cards and I didn't join them often, but I had gone that night."

"Gone where? Whose house?"

Ralph frowned and looked off to the side. "I think his name was Mike. Mike, uh, Mayer or no, Meyers. Something like that. I didn't know him well, but he was a plumber working on the same job as me. He offered to host the group that night, so I went."

"Where did he live?"

"Down Curry Court. I don't remember the number. That was too many years ago." Ralph shook his head in regret.

"He lived in one of the mobile homes in that trailer park? Did Olive know where you were, I mean, the exact address? If she had needed you, could she have reached you?"

"Aw, sure. Maybe she didn't know the number, but she knew I was in the trailer court all right. We didn't carry cell phones back then, but I probably left her a phone number for Mike. I don't remember exactly. It wasn't like I went over there a bunch 'cause he wasn't a regular worker. I only saw him once in a while."

"So, Mike was hired from the Plumber's

Union Hall? You think I can find him if I contact the union office?"

"I don't know. I guess. I didn't get involved in hiring folks, so I don't know how they go about it."

"What job were you working on back then?"

"I don't remember the job site. I might have been in between jobs."

"Who paid your wages? Did you work for a construction company?"

"My, oh my! That's a lot of detail for that long ago." Ralph rubbed his hand over his face.

"I just assumed, since your wife had a fatal accident that night, that you'd probably remember where you were when you found out."

"Yeah, I do, but I was back home before I heard about it."

"Oh! So, the police couldn't locate you that night at all?"

"They were at the house when I got home! That sure gave me a fright. I pulled up about one o'clock, and there were a couple of police cars in the front drive, and the boys were scared to death. It was a horrible scene."

"No one else there? Just the boys?"

"And Billy Nash." Ralph sneered. "That's Marty's dad. I guess he called him."

"Most likely the police asked them to call a friend or family member. They wouldn't have wanted to leave the boys home alone."

Ralph shrugged his acceptance of that answer, but there was no love lost between Ralph and Billy.

"So, you show up and the police tell you what happened, right?"

Ralph nodded.

"What happened next?"

"Well, I sent Billy home and the police talked to me outside. Then we went inside and told the boys." Ralph nodded as if he thought he had that right.

"So, Billy didn't know?"

Ralph looked down at the table. "I don't think so, not until we told the boys, but I know

Marty went in the kitchen and called him right after." Ralph's face heated and his voice raised. "I told him to get off the phone when I heard him in there crying to his daddy. It weren't no business of Billy's."

Conrad's forehead furrowed. "If the circumstances were in reverse, don't you think Douglas would have wanted to reach out to you?"

Ralph sniffed and leaned back in his chair. "I guess. I just got tired of Billy Nash sniffin' around my house all the time."

Conrad reached for the file at the side of the table and slid the manila folder over in front of him. He had sorted things in the order he wanted to present them. Sliding the first photo out with his fingertips, he twisted the photo around to face Ralph. "This is the photo the officers took at the scene. You may have seen this before."

Ralph pulled it closer and leaned over it. "I remember that old car. It worried me for Olive to drive it. It had been making noise and didn't seem right. I told that boy of hers to take it down to the shop and have it looked at. He never listened to me, though. He always knew better."

"The car was in disrepair?" Conrad frowned. "Did Olive know that?"

"I told her it was a shakin' when I drove it and that we needed to have it looked at. I drove my old work truck because I didn't want to risk takin' that car south of town."

"You said 'that boy of hers', do you mean Marty Nash?"

"Yeah, he always worked on cars, and I told him he needed to quit tinkerin' with it and take it down to Wade's for someone to check it out."

"Did the police tell you what caused the accident?" Conrad sat down across from Ralph and leaned forward on his elbows.

"Not directly. It's a bad curve. I expect they thought she took the curve too fast." Ralph tossed his hands up and let them fall lightly on the tabletop. "She wasn't the best driver."

“Did they ask you why she was out there?”

“They did, but I don’t have no idea. She never said she was going anywhere that night.”

“Who did she know that lived out there?” Conrad raised his eyebrows.

“Oh, Olive knew the whole town!” Ralph smiled. “Everyone loved her. It could have been anyone. One of those schoolteacher friends or play people. She always volunteered for different things. I couldn’t keep up with all her happenings.”

“So, you never found out? Those friends never came forward to tell someone she was coming to their house? I would have thought that would be the talk of the town!”

Ralph huffed and shuffled his weight in his chair.

“Well, I guess there was talk around town, though.” Conrad smirked. “Surely, you heard it.”

Ralph sneered. “I don’t visit the gossip circles in this town.”

“Well, I can tell you the speculation by the

general population is that Olive was headed to Nancy's house, because you were there or because she wanted to talk to her about you."

"Nasty scuttlebutt. You know that doesn't hold any water."

"I'm not a Spicetown native, but oftentimes I find the town's moral compass to be pretty spot on, and I can't ignore that."

"Well, I can tell you one thing, Nancy didn't have nothing to do with Olive's accident."

"So, it's a mystery? After twenty years, you still don't have any peace of mind about where she was going or what caused this horrible loss?" Conrad leaned forward, tipping his head down slightly, and looked up at Ralph. "That would put a twist in my gut, I think, but everybody copes differently."

Conrad slid the next picture out of the folder of the car on the flatbed tow truck and turned it around in front of Ralph. "I can tell you that Olive was not impaired in any way, if that puts your mind at ease. No drugs or alcohol influenced her accident. They always check that sort of thing because it is the number one cause for too many dangerous mishaps."

Ralph nodded and looked down at the photo. "If I had to guess, and I hate to say this, but it had to be the boy." Ralph heaved his chest out with a deep breath. "A heavy burden to carry, and I expect he's labored with guilt."

"Which boy?"

"That boy of hers, Marty. It had to be his negligence, but I never wanted to lay that blame on a young'un'."

"So, you feel that Marty Nash is responsible because he didn't get the car checked out?" Conrad's nose wrinkled.

"He was always tinkerin' with that car. He thought he was a great mechanic, but he was just a boy and shouldn't of been messin' around with it all the time."

"And Douglas, the younger son? Was he a mechanic, too?" Conrad stood up and grabbed the back of the chair.

"No. He never had any interest that way." Ralph shook his head and dabbed his handkerchief around his neck. "He wouldn't know a fuel pump from a spark plug."

"Really? I was told he was out in the yard working on the car before the accident." Conrad rubbed his neck. "I've got an eyewitness that says he was adjusting the tires on the car."

"You better double check that source." Ralph scowled and leaned on his elbow to shift his weight in the chair. "That's a lie. Douglas never touched that car, and he wasn't even home that weekend. He was on a trip with the Eagle Scouts. They were at a museum in the city."

"Who do you suppose they saw in the yard?" Conrad tilted his head and furrowed his brow waiting for a reply, but Ralph stared down at the table. "Tell you what, you think on that a bit. I've got something I want to check on. I'll be right back."

Sheri Richey

# Chapter 24

"Look!" Peggy waved Arlene over furiously. "He's got the dress over his arm."

Douglas Vogel stomped across Fennel Street with the blue chiffon dress covered in plastic. He had come from the community center and was angling across the street toward the barbershop.

"He looks mad." Arlene winced.

"I don't know what he's going to do with it." Peggy rolled her eyes. "I don't know why he can't just let the girl wear it in the play. "

"I think it's just a lover's spat. He's a troubled person."

"Look, he's throwing it in the car. Do you know where he lives?" Peggy stepped back when she heard the door to the barbershop slam shut. "Is he living here in town or in Red River?"

"I think he's west of town toward Red River." Arlene jumped when she heard noise against the wall. "It sounds like he's breaking things over there."

"Here he comes." Peggy whispered, as if Doug could hear her. "He put another bag in his car. I think he's leaving."

"I wonder if he had to fight with Eleanor. She might have put up a fuss with him trying to take a costume with the play opening tonight."

"I'm going to follow him." Peggy handed Arlene her pricing gun and grabbed her purse from behind the counter. "I want to see where he's going."

"What? Oh, he might see you. He's already mad. I don't think that's a good idea!" Arlene held up a finger as Peggy pulled the front door open.

“I’ll be right back.” Still whispering, Peggy pulled the door closed quietly and walked down to where her car was parked on Fennel Street. Arlene had parked in the back today so they could load the dog crate in her car. The street parking gave Peggy a clear view of Doug’s little compact car sitting in front of Chervil Drugs.

Peggy started her car and waited. The barbershop door was open, so she knew he was carrying something out to his car and wanted to be ready when he pulled out. Startled by the ringing phone, Peggy saw Arlene’s name on the display. “Hello.”

“Where are you? I can’t see your car.”

“I’m in the next block. I can see his car. It looks like he’s locking up now.”

“Yes, he has a book under his arm. It’s thick, maybe a catalog or something. He seems to be calming down some.”

“I’m just going to follow for a bit and see where he goes. He might be going to Ralph’s. That’s not far. I’ll call you back.” Peggy put the phone in her lap and slowly pulled out, keeping her distance, but with an eye on his car.

Doug drove straight down Fennel Street, turning south on Paprika Parkway, where he gradually increased his speed. Peggy realized they were leaving Spicetown, but there wasn't anywhere to stop or turn around on the highway until they reached the Spicetown Rock Quarry, so she committed to driving that far. The rock quarry was closed on Saturday, so the tall gates were locked up tight, blocking the parking lot. She had to pass by, but slowed because there was a feed store and mobile home park right around the bend in the road.

When Doug slowed his car at the feed store lot, she bit her lip and made a snap decision to pull in. She was afraid he was pulling over because he knew she was back there, but she would just tell him she was there to get the puppy some food.

As she pulled through the gravel parking lot, planning to park right in front of the store, Doug's car turned into the Curry Court Trailer Park. She stopped in front of the store and watched him drive down the middle of the road, slowing to a crawl as he eased his small car over the speed humps in the road. Pulling to the right side, he turned into a short driveway beside a mobile home, and she watched to see if he was going inside.

Peggy went inside the feed store and bought a small bag of puppy food. She wanted her cover story to be good in case she was caught, and since the little snickers bar was spending the night with her, she might actually need it. When she returned to her car, she saw the small blue car hadn't moved, so she decided to risk discovery and drive through the park. There was a circle drive at the back so she could make two passes seamlessly, and she knew Wilma Cooper lived down there. If she had to find a reason for her whereabouts, she was ready with a story. Conrad had taught her to think ahead.

As she passed the trailer, the front door was closed. Doug Vogel must live here, after all. When the phone rang in her lap, she grabbed it to silence it. "Hello."

Her heart was pounding, and she laughed from the tension. "Arlene! The phone scared me."

"Where are you? Are you okay? You said you'd call!"

"I'm fine. I just got the little doodle bug some pup food and drove by Doug's trailer. It looks like he lives out at Curry Court."

"Curry Court! Are you coming back now?"

When she saw Doug's front door open, Peggy pulled her truck over in front of a trailer that looked empty a few doors down. Watching, she whispered into the phone. "I've got to go. He's coming out." She heard Arlene protest, but stopped the call anyway and ducked down, faking a search of her floorboard.

Peggy muttered under her breath when the phone rang again and smacked the phone to answer it. "I'll be back in a few minutes." Peggy's whisper was raspy. Even though it was irrational, she felt that making noise was going to reveal her snooping.

"Peggy?"

Peggy jerked her head back and looked at the phone. "Chief! I didn't know it was you. I thought it was Arlene. I'm sorry."

"That's okay. Are you all right?"

"Oh, yeah. I'm fine. What's going on?"

"Well, I was just calling to see if you had any idea where I might find Doug Vogel. I know you talked to him at the barbershop. Did he mention where he lives or did Nancy tell you?"

"I'm looking at him right now." Peggy turned sideways in her truck to keep Doug from seeing her face and slipped on a ball cap she found behind her seat. "He's at 114 Curry Court and I think he might live here."

"What are you doing there?" Conrad motioned across the lobby for Officer Tabor to come closer. "Are you okay?"

"Yeah, I'm in my truck parked across from him."

"But why? Why are you out there?" Conrad shook his head when he realized she had him whispering unnecessarily, too. "Does he know you're out there?"

"No! I tailed him from the store. I wanted to see where he was going. He went over to the community center and made them give him the dress back. Then he stormed off down the road, so I followed him."

"I'm sending an officer out there to bring him in. You need to get out of there if you can do that without being seen. I don't want him to see you and think you're involved." Conrad wrote the address on his notepad and handed it to Eugene Tabor. Covering his phone receiver with his hand, he said, "Doug Vogel. Bring him in for me."

Eugene nodded and turned to go out the door.

"He looks like he might be getting ready to leave again. He just came out with a box and left his front door opened."

"Tabor is already on his way. Be careful."

"I will be." Peggy sat up and looked down at her phone, scrolling to keep her face down and sneaking a peek when she thought it was safe. Within a few minutes, Officer Tabor pulled into Curry Court and stopped beside Doug's car. Peggy couldn't hear them, but she could see the tension in Doug's body language. At first, he seemed wary, but then he became insistent that he wanted to go. As he walked around the police car, Peggy thought she had been spotted, but Doug got in his car and Officer Tabor turned around to follow him back to town.

Peggy removed the ball cap, fluffed her hair, and started her truck to return to the store. She would have to plan better next time and include some disguises in her glove box for future spy maneuvers.

---

"Afternoon, Ms. Quinn. It's Chief Harris. Is Marty Nash there?"

"Well, howdy, Chief. He surely is. I'll get him for you."

Conrad heard Ella call to Marty as Officer

Tabor stuck his head around the door frame of his office door and held up two fingers to indicate he had secured Doug Vogel in Interview Room Two.

"Hi, Chief. How can I help you?"

"Marty! Hey, I've got Ralph and Doug at the station right now and I have a few questions for you. Your mom's accident was on a Monday night. Do you remember the weekend before? Were you at home? Was everyone home that weekend?"

"I was spending weekends at my dad's a lot back then. I'm sure I was at Wade's on Saturday because my dad worked Saturdays and I went down there to hang out."

"What about Doug? Would he have been home?"

"I don't know where else he would go. He didn't really have many friends or do anything. He was only 13."

"Was he active with any groups that might have had a party or event, like church groups or scouts? Did he go to the movies or anything like that? I don't know, what was a normal weekend around your house like back then?"

"He played video games and watched movies. He never went anywhere. I don't remember anybody being gone that weekend."

"What about Ralph? Did he usually go out on the weekends? You mentioned he went fishing sometimes with Pete. Did he go outside to do yard work, or do you think they might have gone out to eat somewhere? I'm just trying to get a picture of what weekends were like at your house?"

"Ralph wasn't around much. Mom usually went to the store, but Ralph always said he was going to have a drink or meet friends in the evening. During the week he was home some nights, but he just watched TV. My dad said he went to the Wasabi Women's Club. He saw him there a few times."

"You said you put the new tires on a few days before the accident and Ralph had driven the car after that. Did you or your mom drive the car after the new tires were on it?"

"Yeah, sure. She drove it to the store, and I drove it down to Wade's Saturday because I had them balance the tires. I didn't notice any problem with the car at all."

"Okay, last question. That Monday, did everyone go to work and school? Would anyone have been home during the day?"

"We all went to school. Mom went early with Mrs. Kent, and we rode the bus. Ralph was at home when we left, but he probably didn't have to work that day. He didn't have work every day in the winter."

"Was Ralph there when you got home from school?"

"I don't remember for sure, but I don't think so."

"Okay, thanks."

"Do you want me to come down there?"

"That's up to you. You can if you like or drop by after work. If I have more questions, I'll call."

# Chapter 25

"Chief," Tabor jumped up from his desk before Conrad could open the door to Interview Room #2. "Before you go in there, I just wanted to tell you.... That trailer didn't look like he was living in it."

Conrad stepped back. "You think it belonged to someone else?"

Tabor shook his head. "It looked like he used it for storage."

Conrad nodded and reached for the doorknob.

"Chief, I saw in the front door when I pulled up. It was standing open and there were clothes hanging all around the room on metal rods, like a store."

"On hangers?" Conrad frowned.

"Yeah! There wasn't any furniture in there at all."

Conrad stared at the floor and rubbed his hand across his forehead.

"I know he's opening the barbershop, but maybe he has another business in mind, or maybe he's selling something online." Tabor shrugged. "I don't know, but there wasn't room in there to sit down. The kitchen looked like it had boxes in it, but the living room was all clothes."

Conrad hummed and reached for the door. "See if you can find anything out about him online. I'll see what I can find out."

Tabor nodded as Conrad turned the doorknob.

"Good afternoon, Doug. I'm Chief Harris. I don't believe we've met." Conrad grabbed the back of a chair and pulled it out to sit down as Doug paced on the other side of the table.

"Have a seat."

"The other officer said my dad was here."

"He is, but I have a few questions for you, if you don't mind."

"Questions for me? Why? What's this about?"

"I'm trying to clear up a few things about your mother's accident. The report is missing some information, and I had hoped your dad could fill it in, but he's having trouble remembering back to that day. I thought maybe you'd be able to help."

Doug pulled out a chair. "I don't know if I can help."

Conrad leaned back and relaxed, relieved that Doug had calmed. "I hate to bring up this time, but can you tell me what you remember about the weekend before? Were you home? Was the whole family home that weekend?"

Doug rubbed his chin and looked off to the side. "I think I was there. Marty was probably at the shop, but I don't remember going anywhere. Mom went to the grocery store and

Dad may have gone out a few times, but I think he was home Sunday. It was rainy, kind of sleeting that day, I think."

Tabor had checked the weather the day of the accident and the temperature was above freezing on Monday but had dropped that night when the accident happened. "What about Monday? Did you go to school? Ride the bus or ride with your mom? How did you get to school usually?"

"Sometimes we rode the bus if Mom was going in real early or if she stayed late. I think that day Mrs. Kent picked us all up so Dad could use the car. Then we rode the bus home because Mom and Mrs. Kent were staying later. She brought home pizza that night. Dad wasn't home for dinner."

"When you and your brother got home from school, was your dad there?"

"No."

"Was the car there?" Conrad leaned forward on his elbow.

"Yeah, he was gone in his truck."

"Okay, that's helpful. Give me just a minute and I'll be back."

Conrad slipped out the door and Tabor looked up from his computer. "I haven't found anything on him."

"Give Ernie Gramble a call out at Curry Court and see if he'll tell you who rents that trailer."

Tabor nodded.

"Oh, and check the weather the weekend before the accident. Doug says it was rainy on Sunday." Conrad walked over to Tabor's desk. "It might have sleeted a little."

Tabor nodded and began typing. "You think the road could have been slick?"

"I just want to see if I'm getting the truth from him. I'm just testing his memory and his honesty a little. I don't think I'm getting truth from Ralph."

"Yeah, looks accurate," Tabor said. "High of 41 and low of 30 that day with intermittent showers."

Conrad nodded. "We probably need to get

Ralph some lunch. I think he'll be here for a while. Why don't you call over to Old Thyme Italian and order a couple of pizzas?"

"Sure, Chief."

Conrad pushed the door open and apologized to Ralph for the delay. "Sorry about that. We put in an order for some lunch if you're hungry. It should be here soon. Now where were we?"

Ralph shrugged.

"The accident was on a Monday. Tell me what you remember about that day. Did you work? Did Olive go to work?"

"I might have had a small job. I don't remember, but there's not much work in February. I'm sure Olive went to school with the boys. I would have remembered if somebody was sick that day."

"Would Olive have taken the car to work?"

"Yeah, she drove the car, and I drove the truck."

"But you mentioned the car had been making a noise."

"I told her that, but she never paid me any mind. The boy neither. I warned them both."

"But you still think she drove the car to work that day?" Conrad leaned back and crossed his arms over his chest with raised eyebrows. "You saw them pull out that morning?"

"No. I'm just saying that's what usually happened. I don't remember that one morning. That was twenty years ago!"

"But I'm assuming it was the last time you saw your wife."

Ralph looked down at the table, nodding and attempting an expression of grief. He must not have taken acting lessons himself because the effort did not look genuine.

"Let me see if I can help you with your memory. The day before the accident, Sunday, everyone was home. The weather was cold and rainy. Olive got some groceries, the boys watched movies and played video games."

Ralph nodded. "That sounds about right."

"Monday morning you told Olive that you

needed the car, so she called a friend to pick her and the boys up for school. You stayed home with both vehicles. The boys rode the bus home from school, but you were gone in the truck when they arrived. Olive's friend brought her home later, and she had picked up pizza on the way home. You weren't there, but Olive and her sons had pizza for dinner."

"Sounds like you don't need me. You've got it all worked out." Ralph sneered and sat back in his chair.

"I know she had called Nancy Whitehead several times that day trying to talk to her about her pregnancy, and she hadn't reached her by the time she got off work. Most likely, that is what took her down Rosemary Road late that night."

"I don't know where you heard that crazy story!"

"I'm not done." Conrad stood up. "During the day, you went outside and removed the lug nuts from her back tire before you drove away in your truck. Now, some think you did it to make Marty look bad, because you resented her oldest son and were jealous of her first husband, but that's only because people around here like to think the best of people. I, on the other hand, think you removed those lug nuts because you hoped for just what happened."

"Now, you wait just a darned minute!" Ralph slammed his fist down on the table and the momentum helped him rise from his seat. "I'm not going to sit here and have you—."

Conrad reached for the doorknob. "You see if that helps your memory any, and I'll check on lunch." Pulling the door shut behind him, he couldn't help but laugh at Ralph's fury.

"Everything okay in there?" Eugene smiled with worry lines across his forehead.

"Oh, yeah. Ralph's just getting some exercise. Are those pizzas coming?"

Eugene checked his watch. "I'll run across the street and get them."

Conrad turned around when he heard knocking on the window of Interview Room #2. "Let me see if Doug is hungry yet?" Tabor left out the side door and Conrad entered the second room.

"Are you hungry, Doug? We're getting some pizza delivered here in a minute."

"Was that my dad? I just heard someone. Where is he?"

"Oh, he's just waiting on the pizzas."

"What was he yelling about? Is he upset? Can I see him?"

"Not just yet. Let him settle a little. He's upset because I told him about what happened that Monday while you were at school. It's got him a bit riled. Have a seat."

"What? What happened that Monday?"

"Do you know what a lug nut is, Doug?"

"It's what holds on a tire."

Conrad nodded. "Have you ever changed a tire, Doug?"

"No, but I've seen it done." Doug took a seat across from Conrad.

"Do you know how they do it? How do you get the lug nuts off?" Conrad held his hands out to encourage Doug to explain.

"You use a wrench." Doug shrugged.

"Does your dad know? Can he change a tire?"

"Yeah. He's done it, when he had to."

"Does he have one of those wrenches?"

"I guess so. I think he keeps that stuff in the trunk with the spare."

"Do you know what those wrenches look like?"

"I don't know. Marty used to do that."

"You ever help him?"

"Nah, I never learned much about cars. That didn't interest me."

"I didn't think so." Conrad shook his head. In the beginning, he had pegged Doug for this foolish prank, thinking his youth didn't afford him the wisdom to weigh the consequences, but now he felt pretty confident that it was Ralph all along. It wasn't easy to loosen those lug nuts, especially after the car had been taken to the garage.

"Your mom's car had new tires that Marty put on it. Did you know that?" Conrad leaned forward and raised his eyebrows. Doug hadn't tried to blame Marty as he had expected.

"Yeah, Dad was worried he hadn't done it right, but Marty did that kind of stuff all the time."

"Did you know Marty took it down to Wade's Garage to have the tires balanced after he put them on?"

"No, but I wouldn't. I mean, it doesn't surprise me that he would do that. He went down there all the time."

"Well, it isn't easy to get lug nuts off when they've been to a shop like that. They put those nuts on with an impact wrench and then tighten them with a torque wrench. It's not like turning a wood screw. There's a special torque, an exact tension that needs to be done. People don't just drive away from tire stores and have tires fall off. Do you know what I mean?"

"Yeah." Doug shrugged. "Mom's tires didn't fall off."

"Actually, one did, and that's what caused her car to veer into that concrete embankment.

While you were at school that day, someone removed the lug nuts from one of the back tires, so when she took that turn out Michaels' Curve, she lost control of the car."

Doug sat back and looked down at his hands in his lap. "Are you trying to say my dad did this?"

"He was at home alone with the car all day." When Doug didn't respond, Conrad stood up. "I'll go check on the pizza. I'll be right back."

Sheri Richey

# Chapter 26

"Can you see all right?" Cora Mae twisted in her chair. She had picked these specific seats in the community center after having tried out several while attending past plays, and these were her favorites. However, something was obstructing her view tonight.

"Yeah, same as always." Conrad leaned toward Cora and saw the probable obstruction. "Bert Miller too tall for you?"

Cora huffed. "He's right in the middle."

"Trade me seats." The lights had flickered a warning that the curtain would go up soon, so he needed to get her settled quickly. Conrad stood and stepped to the side while she moved over. “Is that better?”

“Yes! Thank you. Did you look at the program?”

“Not yet.” Conrad opened it and looked down at the list of names. “I guess that girl was right. Saucy is the director.” Chuckling, he glanced at Cora Mae and pointed to the program. “See, it says so right here.”

“That doesn’t make any sense. Why would a play about a millionaire and his family have a role for a director. Director of what, I wonder.”

“Maybe it’s a hospital director or something. Doesn’t the guy die?”

“That could be.” Cora nodded. “It must be a small role because I never saw him do anything at practices.”

“He probably needs a break from all that memorizing and all that anxiety he would work up before each show. Maybe this time, he can relax and enjoy it. Did he come by your office with butterflies in his stomach again this time?”

“No! No, he didn’t. You’re right. He’s always aflutter before each opening night. He must feel pretty confident this time."

"Or he's just not going to give away his secret to you. He always wants to surprise you."

Cora Mae chuckled. "He does, but he just doesn't understand how much anxiety that gives me!"

"I know you hate a secret!"

"Speaking of secrets, what was the end result today? Did you arrest anyone after all that talking?"

"No, I didn't, but I kicked it over to the prosecutor's office so they can decide what to do. Ralph insists he didn't mean to put anyone in danger. He had planned to just show it to Olive to convince her that Marty shouldn't be allowed to work on the car anymore. He never thought she'd try to drive it that night."

"It has been twenty years and the investigation that should have happened back then didn't get done properly."

"That's true. I don't think they'd be able to charge him with murder with what I have, but he is confessing to tampering with her vehicle.

Maybe the county will re-open the case. The statute of limitations for involuntary manslaughter is 20 years in Ohio, though, so unless they can prove murder, he won't be charged."

"At least the boys know, although it must be heartbreaking to hear. The family may be more fractured than ever."

"Actually, it seems to have brought Doug and Marty together. Doug wanted to support his dad, but after this came out, he loved his mom too much to rationalize it all. He doesn't blame Marty. I was afraid he might twist it to think Marty's relationship with Ralph made Ralph do it, but he didn't look at it that way. Marty showed up at the station when he got off work and Doug asked to talk to him. He wanted to tell Marty what his dad had done. I was worried that Marty wouldn't take it well from him either. Marty could have blamed Doug because it was his dad, but Marty's got a pretty clear head now. He's come to terms with his past, and I think maybe some good came from all this."

"Maybe Doug and Marty can be each other's family from now on." Cora clasped her hands in her lap.

"Maybe. I do think Doug needs some counseling. Hoarding all of his mother's things in storage is a sure sign that he hasn't managed her death well." Conrad did feel a burden lifted just in the knowing. He hoped they did, too. A death should never be accepted without the cause examined, even if it did happen over twenty years ago.

"I'm glad Peggy took the steps to bring it up and make us all take a closer look. I've never known her to get involved in anything like this before."

Conrad chuckled. "Yeah, finding that dress lit a fire under her. She's got a little sleuth in her, too."

"What do you mean, too?" Cora Mae widened her eyes innocently. "We are just curious people!"

"That you are!" Conrad nodded curtly.

"Shh, it's starting. Look, it's Saucy. He's starting the show! Look at that cute little hat!"

Cora Mae sat quietly until intermission, and then she wanted to squeal. "Eleanor is a genius! This is the perfect place for Saucy. He should narrate all the plays! He gets to hold a clipboard and read his part, and he's so cute. I wonder if she thought this up or if the play is really written this way."

Conrad nodded his head in agreement. If the role was intended as a confused director who did not know how the play was going to turn out, Saucy was perfect casting.

"And we get to vote on the killer. Did you hear that? This is such fun! Who do you think did it?"

"We haven't even seen all the actors yet. Fred Rucker plays the detective, which is probably why we have to decide who the murderer is." Conrad laughed.

"Well, so far I'm leaning toward one of those Arnett girls." Cora Mae frowned. "Nina is my first pick."

"Now, don't let your personal feelings get involved." Conrad smiled. "Is there really an answer, or does the majority win? That part wasn't clear to me."

"You'll just have to wait and see." Cora Mae smugly imitated Conrad, who always wanted her to wait for secrets to be revealed. "Jimmy Kole is doing a great job as the butler. I know he wanted to be the millionaire, but this role is much more demanding. Maybe he should have been an actor instead of a city councilman." Cora shrugged her shoulders innocently.

"Who knew?" Conrad laughed.

"Oh! I was talking to someone over at the courthouse in Paxton today, and there is a rumor that a new business is buying up that wooded land just outside our city limits on the road to Paxton. They didn't know who it was, but thought it was some big developer."

"That might be what you need to bring shoppers to the area."

Cora stretched her back one more time as the light flickered for people to return to their seats for the second half of the play. "Keep your ear to the ground and let me know if you hear anything about it!"

---

"This has been a crazy day. Do you think our neighbor will be okay?" Arlene glanced at the adjoining wall. Cora Mae had called the store and told Peggy about Ralph Vogel's confession and thanked Peggy for her help.

"It depends on how he handles the information that his father basically killed his mom.

"Are you sure you're going to be okay?" Arlene wrung her hands in worry. Peggy was a cat person. She wasn't sure the puppy going home with Peggy was such a great idea after all.

"I've got this." Peggy brushed her concerns away with a wave of her hand. "I'll put him in this box while I drive, and I can block him off in the utility room for the night. I can put papers down. There's no carpeting in there, just laundry stuff.

"Do you have something for him to sleep on? He needs a blanket or towels, something soft."

"I'll figure it out. I've got his leash in my purse and his food is in the car."

"Now, he'll have to go outside after he eats and again before bedtime."

Peggy nodded. "Do you have to burp him after he eats?"

"Oh, you!"

Peggy laughed at Arlene's bluster. "We'll be fine. I don't have any big plans for tomorrow. I'm just going to relax. We'll see you Monday."

Arlene nodded.

"Unless, of course, I've lost him by then." Peggy cackled as she walked out the door and Arlene yelled at her.

"You be careful with little Bubba."

"See you Monday." Peggy pushed the box

full of bossy pup into the passenger seat and fastened her seatbelt. The pup instantly stood on his hind legs and scratched to be released.

"Shh, now. We just have a short drive, and you can't be running around while I'm driving." Keeping her right hand in the box, rubbing the puppy's ears and driving with her left hand, she pulled her car into the garage and began to unload while the puppy protested the lack of attention.

Settling in the kitchen, Peggy grabbed a cereal bowl and poured out some puppy food, using another cereal bowl as a water bowl. Then she went in search of towels or blankets. "Don't you wander off. I'll be right back."

When she returned, the little runt was sniffing around the kitchen and she scooped him up to take him outside, where he continued to explore, but eventually got his job accomplished. Back inside, she took the pup to the laundry room, showed him his water bowl and his sleeping pallet, then blocked him in the room with a laundry basket and a kitchen chair.

Setting out to make herself a bite to eat, the puppy began to whine, softly at first, with a heartbreaking bequest and then escalating to an urgent indignant yip yap! Her nervousness at handling this pup on her own had destroyed her appetite, and she began to doubt her ability to get through the rest of the weekend. What if he barked all night? She should have asked Arlene how to soothe him. He couldn't run free throughout the house. What if he hurt himself? Her house wasn't puppy proof! This was a miserable idea. The things you do for a friend...

Collecting her plate and drink, she moved to the living room and turned on the television with plans to drown out the crying and hope the pup settled in for the night, but her hopes disintegrated when she heard the scratching as the pup tried to claw his way out. Frustrated and nervous, she put up her dishes and picked up the pup, carrying him to her recliner. "Let's sit here and watch this movie. You have to be still and behave."

The pup planted himself on her lap like a

water balloon, wobbling all around with each breath, nudging his nose one way, then the other until he settled into a comfortable spot. As he fell into a deep sleep, he began to whistle from his tiny pink nose. However cute it was, it would probably turn into a big dog snore soon enough. Stroking his wrinkled face and velvety ears, she tried to imagine him fully grown, fat and bossy. He lacked the quiet dignity that her cat, Lolly, had always shown. He would probably drool and snort along with other rude things, and he might even be a little ugly by some perceptions, but he'd had a hard beginning. Left at the trash dumpster in an alley is not a confident start, even for a wrinkly pup.

Arlene was right. He needed a permanent home and people he could call his own. He needed a regular place to sleep and a proper name. She didn't know if she could give him any of that, but Peggy had to admit she liked having the little fur ball asleep in her lap. Maybe with Arlene's help they could train him to behave at the store and she wouldn't have to come home alone anymore.

He'd been called a lot of different names in the last few days. Many of those names described his physique or his attitude accurately, but none of those names meant family. From this night on, Peggy decided that this little tootsie roll, wooly worm, biscuit buster would now be called Sully. That had been her father, John Sullivan's, nickname, and now it would belong to the new man in her life, and they would be family, even if he did snore.

Sheri Richey

**Next in the Carom Seed Cozy Series:**

**Read the first chapter here:**

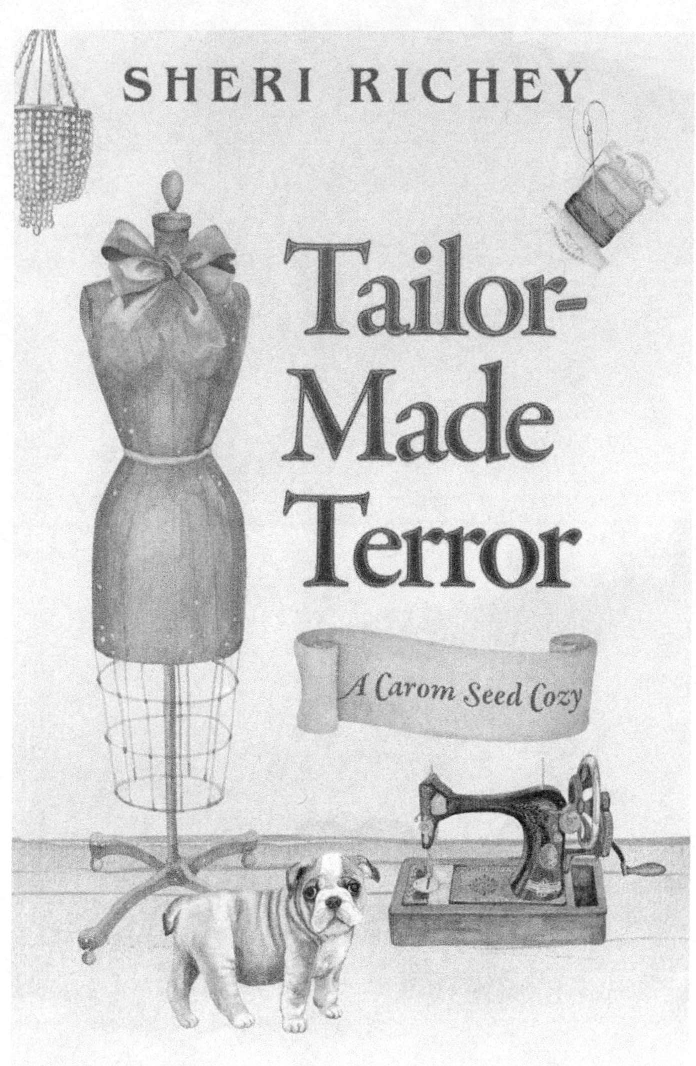

Sheri Richey

# Chapter 1
# Tailor-Made Terror

Cora Mae Bingham struggled to get inside the first set of glass doors to the Caraway Cafe with her umbrella. As helpful as they were, umbrellas became her enemy when she tried to get in or out of anywhere. Fluffing her hair and stomping her feet, she stood the umbrella in the corner declaring victory and exhaled loudly before calmly entering the restaurant.

"Oh, dear. I know I'm late, but it has been a whirlwind of a morning!" Cora pulled out the chair opposite Police Chief Conrad Harris and flopped down hard into the seat.

"Well, my morning has been rather droll." Conrad chuckled. "What's going on at city hall?"

"Amanda and I have been in a dither all day." Cora ordered some hot tea from the waitress and straightened her jacket lapel. "I've got good news, which has put a dozen things on my to-do list, and potentially bad news, which is something you have to keep secret. Which do you want to hear first?"

Conrad furrowed his brow as he weighed the options. "Let's start off on a good note."

"Okay!" Cora Mae thanked the young girl for the hot water and dropped her tea bag into her cup. "Sonjay Wilson called. He's going to loan us his Spicetown collection for display. We can only have the paintings for a week because he has another gallery showing scheduled mid-month, but he is sending them to us today. I'm going to put them up in the community center and Amanda is writing a press release so we can let people know about it. After they arrive, she's going to photograph them for the website, too. I'm so excited to see them!"

"Tabor has seen some of them online." Officer Eugene Tabor had his nose in his phone constantly, but he kept Conrad informed.

"Amanda has seen the photos he shares with Bryan. She says he's working on seasons now, so there will be a Spicetown Autumn series and then winter. They are selling well, so he's considering doing some with holiday themes, too."

"I'm glad he's doing well." Conrad smiled at the waitress when she approached them to order and they both ordered the special of the day, the Chicken Breast Croissant Sandwich.

"Peggy has the community center booked next week, so I've got to talk to her about re-arranging things. I hope she hasn't already advertised the event. I'm hoping she might want to help. We'll need to extend the viewing hours and I'll need someone to oversee things. Gloria can work down there during the day. Amanda said she or Bryan would cover a couple of nights, but the weekend is a challenge."

"Are you going to need security? I might need to put someone on duty there in the evenings if you are staying open at night."

"Maybe until eight o'clock. I'll let you know when I work it all out." Cora Mae leaned away from the table as the waitress brought the lunch platters to the table. "I haven't seen Dorothy. Is she here?"

"Yes, she's in the kitchen helping Mr. Parish. Jason is off today." The young girl looked a bit harried. Dorothy usually helped on the floor with the lunch rush, so the servers were taxed today. "Can I get you anything else?"

Conrad shook his head and thanked the young woman before draping his napkin in his lap. "Okay, so I'm ready. Hit me with the bad stuff."

Cora Mae chuckled. "Well, you have to keep it quiet, but I talked to my friend, Julie, at the county clerk's department today and I asked her about the sale of that land just outside the city limits on the east side. You know, the rumors were that there was a big corporation that bought all that undeveloped land, and we had hoped it was for a retail establishment."

Conrad nodded as he chewed.

"It was bought by a corporation called BonLark, Incorporated, which I have never heard of, so Amanda started digging online."

Conrad frowned. "So, what does this BonLark do?"

"Well, that's really not clear. Amanda says it is two men that just partnered up to create this new corporation, but in the past they both were involved with big companies, just not together."

"Maybe they're both going to try something new. Those big money people can have their hands in lots of different things. They like to diversify."

Cora Mae hummed. "Amanda is worried because they are going to need to clear-cut dozens of acres of forest and the wildlife will be displaced. I'm all for bringing jobs to the community, but not if it means a smelly eyesore on the edge of town."

"Is it a done deal already?"

"No, she said the sale was pending some

kind of permit approval and that part hasn't gone through yet. That's all she knew."

Conrad brushed crumbs from his fingers. "So, how are you going to find out? I know you won't be able to stand not knowing."

"Amanda's checking on the land. I don't know who owns it anymore. It used to belong to Marvin Goddard, but I'm pretty sure he sold it when he retired to move to Florida. I don't know who he sold it to, though. If it's someone I know, maybe they can tell me what this corporation wants to do there."

"Sounds like a good plan."

When they finished eating, Cora decided to walk down to the Carom Seed Craft Corner before returning to City Hall. It was just a block down and the rain was only a sprinkle now.

"Afternoon, ladies!" Cora Mae called out to Peggy and Arlene as the bells attached to the front door jangled. When a small yap sounded, Cora stepped back with her hand over her heart.

"Sully apologizes," Peggy said, frowning

down at the puppy at her feet. "We are still working on a proper greeting."

"Proper or not, it is unique!" Cora Mae smiled. "Hi, Arlene. How are you both?"

"We're doing great, Cora. What are you up to today?" Arlene picked up Sully and put him back in his crate with a toy.

"I have news!" Cora clapped her hands together and told them both about the art exhibit coming to town.

"I haven't advertised the craft weekend yet, so there should be no problem delaying it to another time." Peggy secretly did a happy dance in her head at the thought of having a relaxing weekend without the additional obligations.

"Well, I was hoping you might want to be involved in some way." Cora tilted her head as Arlene straightened her back and raised her finger in the air.

"We could paint, too!" Arlene's excitement was met with bewilderment.

"We don't have paints, Arlene, and I can't

paint." Peggy shook her head.

"How do you know? Have you tried it? It'll be fun. We can learn, too, and there's plenty of time to buy some paint. I'll run to Paxton and pick some up."

"But we don't have an instructor unless you can teach people how to paint."

Cora stepped forward. "Amanda might do it. I could ask her."

"There you go! Problem solved." Arlene held her arm out toward Cora. "I'll call her, and she can tell me what kind of paint to get. I don't know anything about painting. Do you think we could section the community center floor off, so we are on one side and the real paintings are protected?"

"I don't exactly know how many we are getting, but I'll know more tomorrow. I think we should be able to do that. I'll need someone to keep an eye on things though. I don't want Sonjay's paintings to be harmed in any way."

Peggy wasn't certain she wanted to be part of this. "Talk to Amanda and see what she thinks first. We'll wait to hear back from you."

"Okay, ladies. You have a good day." Cora waved as she stepped out the door.

Peggy spun around to face Arlene. "We can't paint. What were you thinking?"

"I'm thinking about ways for you to make money!"

"Buying paints retail and selling them at cost does not make me money." Peggy sat down behind the counter. "I was looking forward to having a peaceful weekend."

"I'm sorry, but if we could find an instructor that's free, you could make money. People that don't usually craft would love to try this."

"Amanda has a business to run. I'm sure Saturdays are busy at the nursery. She won't want to do this."

"There are other people we could ask." Arlene wrinkled her brow in thought.

"Who?" Peggy smirked.

"Doreen! I think she paints with acrylics and Miriam. I think she does watercolors."

“Miriam Landry! Are you kidding me? She doesn’t do anything for free.”

“You’ve got a point.” Arlene lowered her head in defeat. “Wait! I think Francine Dobbs paints landscapes, flowers, and such. I’ll give her a call right now.”

Peggy sighed. “Maybe just one class. Ask her if she’ll do a painting class at one o’clock. That way we aren’t there all day long.”

Arlene nodded and pulled her mobile phone from her pocket while Peggy put her cross stitch project in a plastic bag. She had been working on a small sample for display for the store, but that would have to wait for later.

When the store phone rang, Peggy grabbed it. “Carom Seed Craft Corner.”

“Peggy? It’s Sally McGivens at the Spicetown Star.”

“Hey, Sally. What’s up?”

“I was calling to see if you were planning an ad for the weekend. I’m saving a place for it, but then I wasn’t sure you needed it.”

“I won’t know for sure until tomorrow.

Cora Mae might be in with an ad she needs to run so save some space for her, too. We are changing things up at the community center this weekend. She's expecting Sonjay Wilson's paintings to arrive, and they'll be on display at the community center this weekend. There might be a painting class with it, but I haven't found anyone to do that yet."

"Wow! I may have to come to that. I'm not crafty, but I'd love to learn to paint." Peggy hated it when Arlene was right.

"I'll let you know."

"Oh, one more thing, and don't hate me for this, but Ed was asking us to recommend someone who could do alterations."

"Oh..."

"I gave him your name and the store number, so he might be calling you."

"Ed Poindexter?"

"Yeah."

"You gave Ed Poindexter my phone number?" Ed was the editor of the Spicetown Star, and Peggy always hid from him when she went over to the newspaper office to set up her ads.

"Yeah. I'm sorry, Peggy. You can always tell him you're booked if you don't want to do it, but he's lost a ton of weight, and he wears very expensive clothes. He needs them all taken in and I'm sure he'll pay you well for your work."

"But he's such a..."

"I know. I know. No one knows that more than me. It's just, well, he asked, and you're the first person I thought of. Like I said, I think he'll pay you well."

Peggy chewed her lip. She could really use the extra money. "Okay. I understand and thanks for thinking about me. I don't think he likes me very much, so I may never hear from him, anyway."

"He doesn't like anyone, Peggy." Sally laughed.

# I'd love to hear from you!

Find me on Facebook, Goodreads, Twitter, my website, or join my email list for upcoming news!

www.SheriRichey.com

If this is your first trip to Spicetown and you would like to see more, you can learn all about the town in the original Spicetown Mystery Series.

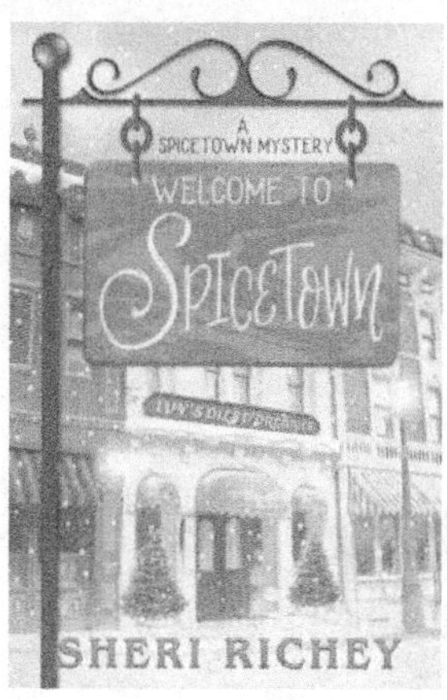

Made in the USA
Monee, IL
24 September 2024